Kelly Regan

Dear Reader,

If you thought there were no more Oz books after the original fourteen by L. Frank Baum, do we have a marvelous treat in store for you. Ruth Plumly Thompson, named the new Royal Historian of Oz after Baum's death, continued the series for nineteen volumes. And we will be reviving these wonderful books, which have been out of print and unattainable anywhere for almost twenty years.

Readers who are familiar with these books swear that they are just as much fun as the originals. Thompson brought to Oz an extra spice of charming humor and an added richness of imagination. Her whimsical use of language and deftness of characterization make her books a joy to read—for adults and children alike.

If this is your first journey into Oz, let us welcome you to one of the most beloved fantasy worlds ever created. And once you cross the borders, beware—you may never want to leave.

Happy Reading,
Judy-Lynn and Lester del Rey

THE WONDERFUL OZ BOOKS
Now Published by Del Rey Books

By L. Frank Baum

#1 The Wizard of Oz
#2 The Land of Oz
#3 Ozma of Oz
#4 Dorothy and the Wizard in Oz
#5 The Road to Oz
#6 The Emerald City of Oz
#7 The Patchwork Girl of Oz
#8 Tik-Tok of Oz
#9 The Scarecrow of Oz
#10 Rinkitink in Oz
#11 The Lost Princess of Oz
#12 The Tin Woodsman of Oz
#13 The Magic of Oz
#14 Glinda of Oz

By Ruth Plumly Thompson

#15 The Royal Book of Oz
#16 Kabumpo in Oz
#17 The Cowardly Lion of Oz
#18 Grampa in Oz
#19 The Lost King of Oz
#20 The Hungry Tiger of Oz
#21 The Gnome King of Oz
#22 The Giant Horse of Oz
#23 Jack Pumpkinhead of Oz
*#24 The Yellow Knight of Oz
*#25 Pirates in Oz
*#26 The Purple Prince of Oz

* Forthcoming

The Gnome King of OZ

by

Ruth Plumly Thompson

Founded on and continuing the Famous Oz Stories

by

L. Frank Baum

"Royal Historian of Oz"

with illustrations by

John R. Neill

A Del Rey Book
Ballantine Books • New York

A Del Rey Book
Published by Ballantine Books

Library of Congress Catalog Card Number: 85-90574

ISBN: 0-345-32358-0

Cover design by Georgia Morrissey
Cover illustration by Michael Herring
Text design by Gene Siegel

Manufactured in the United States of America

First Ballantine Books Edition: October 1985

10 9 8 7 6 5 4 3 2 1

This Book Is Dedicated to My Nephew
Richard Shuff Thompson, Jr.

With lots of love and a little laugh,
For a little boy almost three and a half!
If I had a wish, I'd wish it quick
And keep him always "Little Dick."

R.P.T.

IMPASSABLE
The MARVELOU
OOGABOO
CORUMBIA
SAMANDRA
CORABIA
Skeezers
Reera
Flathead Mt.
Mist Valley
Quick City
Parashuter
(Subterranea-U)
Double Up
Spiders
Ozwoz
GILLIKIN
Stiff R.
Gamer R.
Kuma Party
Jack Pott
PATCH
Great Gillikin Forest
Forest of Gugu
Backwoods
Scooters
Soap Slide
Suds
Dangerous Passage
Bewilderness
Buttonwood
KIMBALOO
Gillikin River
Hoopers
Laughing Willows
Somewhere
Inland Sea
Catty Corners
Blankenburg
DEADLY DESERT
Wish Way
Sun Top Mt.
Tune Town
Pokes
Candy Giant
Fix City
Twigs
Road
Kite Is.
Hidden Valley
Equinots
Dr. Nikidik
Mombi
Shadow Mt.
Winkie River
WINKIE
Ice town
Book-ville
Serpent Tree
Marsh land
Loonville
Perhaps City
Maybe Mts.
Play City
Witch of the West
Monday Mt.
Wish Way
Tree of Whutter Wee
Village of Field Mice
Squirrel King
Black Forest
Mt. Much
Tin Woodman's Castle
Jack Pumpkinhead
EMER CIT
Scarecrow's Tower
Wise Acres
Lake Quad
River
Ugu
Great Orchard
Merry-Go-Round Mts.
Rolling Prairie
Herku
Thi
Winkie River
COUNTRY
Bear Center
Tottenhots
Flutterbudgets
Scare City
Chimneyville
Utensia
Bunbury
River
White Woods
Bottles
Up & Down Waterfall
Trick River
Hoppers
Horners
Rigmarole Town
Swing City
Big Enough (Loxo)
Little Enough
Bourne
Land of the Barons
Red Mts.
Based on the Original Map drawn by Professor H.M.WOGGLEBUG,T.E.
Revised in accordance with the Royal Histories of OZ
N
W
E
S
Z
Big Top Mt.
Baffleburg
Lollypop Village
QUADLING
Ruby Imp's Cavern
Carrot Mt.
Twinlet Town
Posties
South Mt.
Dark Forest
Truth Pond
YIPS
JAMES E. HAFF Delineavit
GREAT
SA

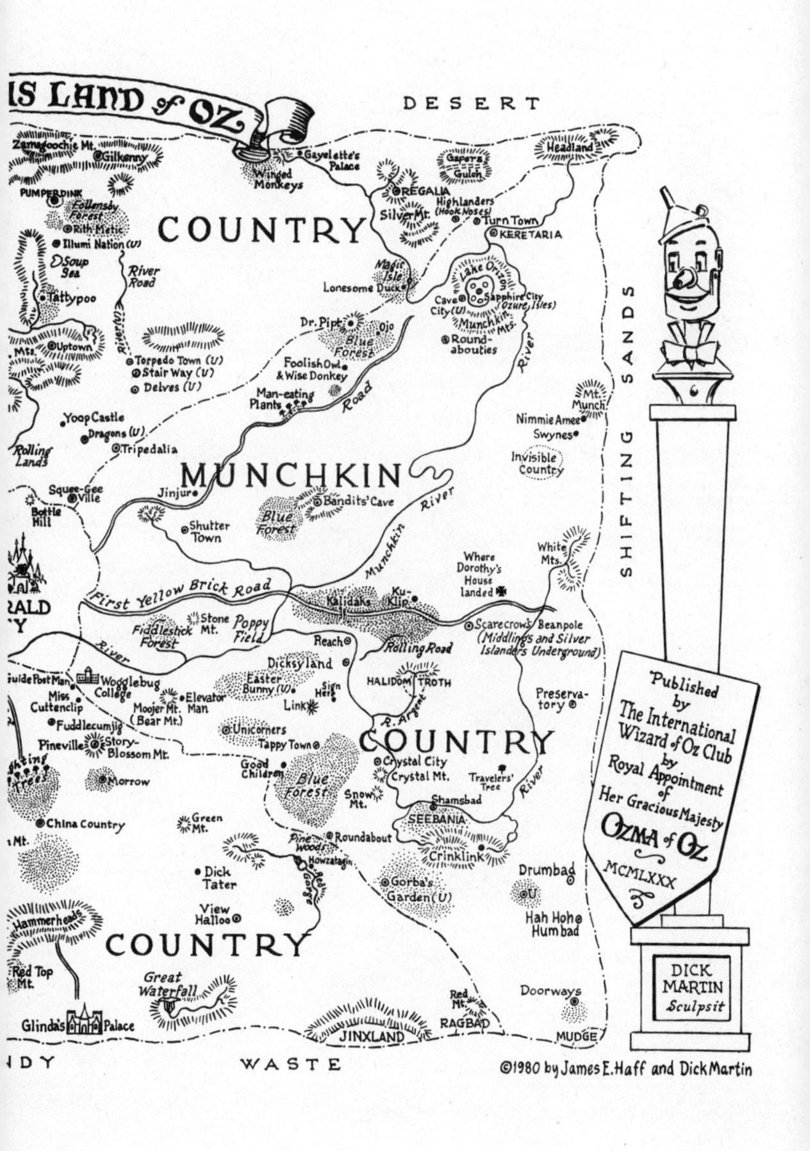

IS LAND of OZ
DESERT
COUNTRY
MUNCHKIN
COUNTRY
COUNTRY
SHIFTING SANDS
WASTE
NDY
Zamagoochie Mt.
Gilkenny
Winged Monkeys
Gayelette's Palace
Gapers Gulch
Headland
REGALIA
Highlanders (Hook Noses)
Silver Mt.
Turn Town
KERETARIA
PUMPERDINK
Follensby Forest
Rith Metic
Illumi Nation (U)
Soup Sea
River Road
Tattypoo
Magic Isle
Lonesome Duck
Lake Orizon
Cave City (U)
Sapphire City (Ozure Isles)
Munchkin Mts.
Round-abouties
Dr. Pipt
Ojo
Blue Forest
Uptown
Torpedo Town (U)
Stair Way (U)
Delves (U)
Foolish Owl & Wise Donkey
Man-eating Plants
Road
River
Yoop Castle
Dragons (U)
Tripedalia
Rolling Lands
Mt. Munch
Nimmie Amee
Swynes
Invisible Country
Squee-Gee Ville
Bottle Hill
Jinjur
Bandits' Cave
Blue Forest
Shutter Town
Munchkin River
Where Dorothy's House landed
White Mts.
First Yellow Brick Road
Kalidahs
Ku-Klip
Stone Mt.
Poppy Field
Fiddlestick Forest
Scarecrow's Beanpole (Middlings and Silver Islanders Underground)
River
Reach
Rolling Road
Dicksyland
HALIDOM
TROTH
Guide Post Man
Wogglebug College
Miss Cuttenclip
Easter Bunny (U)
Sign Here
Link
Elevator Man
Moojer Mt. (Bear Mt.)
Preserva-tory
R. Argent
Fuddlecumjig
Unicorners
Tappy Town
Pineville
Story-Blossom Mt.
Crystal City
Crystal Mt.
Good Children
Blue Forest
Snow Mt.
Travelers' Tree
River
Morrow
Shamsbad
SEEBANIA
China Country
Green Mt.
Pine Woods
Roundabout
Crinklink
Howzatagin
Red Gorge
Dick Tater
Gorba's Garden (U)
Drumbad
Hah Hoh Humbad
View Halloo
Hammerheads
Red Top Mt.
Great Waterfall
Doorways
Red Mt.
RAGBAD
Glinda's Palace
JINXLAND
MUDGE
Published by The International Wizard of Oz Club by Royal Appointment of Her Gracious Majesty OZMA of OZ
MCMLXXX
DICK MARTIN Sculpsit

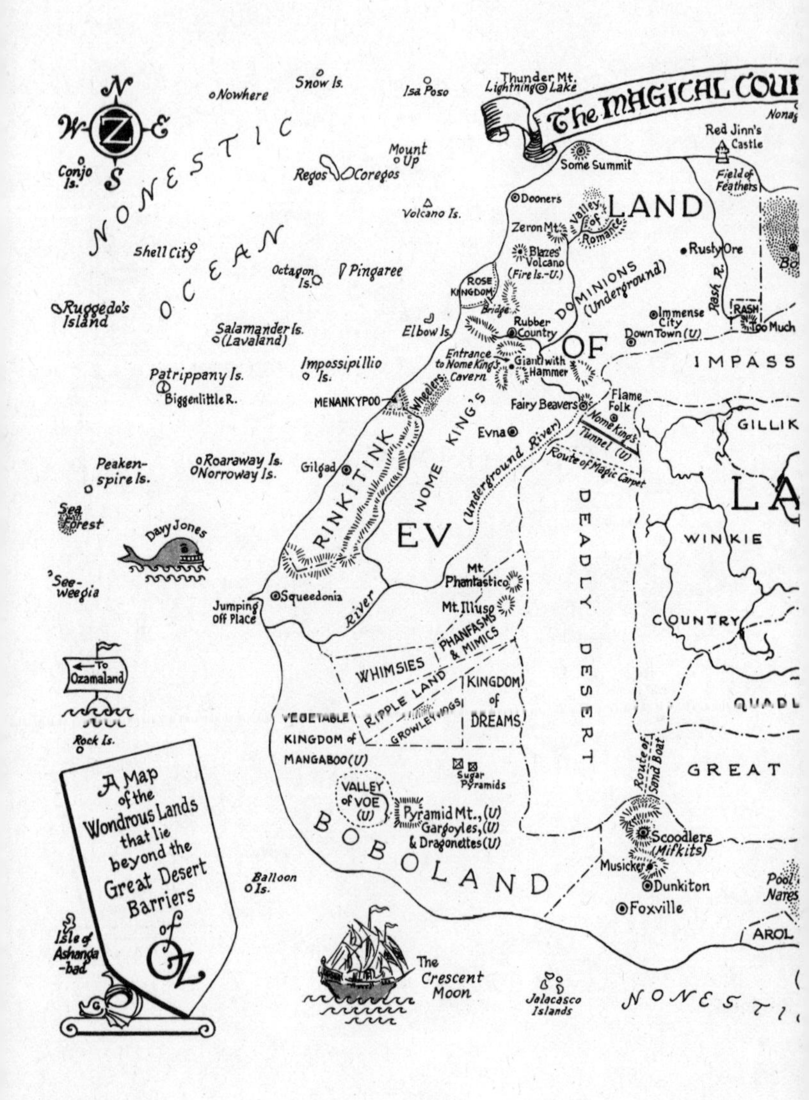

The MAGICAL COU
A Map of the Wondrous Lands that lie beyond the Great Desert Barriers of OZ
NONESTIC OCEAN
Nowhere
Snow Is.
Isa Poso
Thunder Mt.
Lightning Lake
Conjo Is.
Mount Up
Regos
Coregos
Volcano Is.
Shell City
Octagon Is.
Pingaree
Ruggedo's Island
Salamander Is. (Lavaland)
Elbow Is.
Patrippany Is.
Biggenlittle R.
Impossipillio Is.
MENANKYPOO
Peakenspire Is.
Roaraway Is.
Norroway Is.
Gilgad
Sea Forest
Davy Jones
See-weegia
Jumping Off Place
Squeedonia
To Ozamaland
Rock Is.
Isle of Ashanga-bad
Balloon Is.
The Crescent Moon
Jalacasco Islands
Some Summit
Red Jinn's Castle
Field of Feathers
Dooners
LAND
Valley of Romance
Zeron Mt.
Blazes' Volcano (Fire Is.-U.)
Rusty Ore
ROSE KINGDOM
Bridge
DOMINIONS (Underground)
Rash R.
Immense City
RASH
Too Much
Rubber Country
Down Town (U)
Entrance to Nome King's Cavern
Giant with Hammer
OF
IMPASS
Wheelers
Fairy Beavers
Flame Folk
Nome King's Tunnel (U)
GILLIK
Evna
NOME KING'S
RINKITINK
(Underground River)
Route of Magic Carpet
LA
EV
DEADLY DESERT
WINKIE
COUNTRY
Mt. Phantastico
Mt. Illuso
PHANFASMS & MIMICS
River
WHIMSIES
RIPPLE LAND
GROWLEYWOGS
KINGDOM of DREAMS
QUADL
VEGETABLE KINGDOM of MANGABOO (U)
Sugar Pyramids
Route of Sand Boat
GREAT
VALLEY of VOE (U)
Pyramid Mt., (U)
Gargoyles, (U)
& Dragonettes (U)
BOBOLAND
Scoodlers (Mifkits)
Musicker
Dunkiton
Foxville
Pool
Nares
AROL
NONESTI

...TRIES surrounding OZ
Roly-Rogues Is.
The Sea Fairies
Isle of Dork
NONESTIC OCEAN
North Mts.
Roly-Rogues
KINGDOM OF IX
City of Ix
NOLAND
Nole
Aquareine's Palace (Undersea)
Valley of Lost Things
SKAMPAVIA
Valley of Toy Animals
Isle of Phreex
Valley of Pussy-cats
MERRY-LAND
Valley of Clowns
Valley of Bonbons
Valley of Dolls
Valley of Babies
River
ABLE DESERT
Palace of Romance
Isle of Mifkets
Pirate Is.
COUNTRY
ND OF OZ
MUNCHKIN
EMERALD CITY
COUNTRY
SHIFTING SANDS
Heelers
LOLAND
HILAND
Lo
Hie
The Enchanted Isle of Yew
Forest of Lurla
HEG
AURIEL
SPOR
DAWNA
Twi
PLENTA
Island of Civilized Monkeys
ORKLAND
ING COUNTRY
KINGDOM of SCOWLEYOW
Mt. Mern
AURISSAU
Fistikins
SANDY WASTE
VALLEY OF MO
(Phunnyland)
Rock Beer R.
Milk R.
Maple Syrup R.
Crystal Lake
Hartilaf
Jackdaws' Nest
RIBDIL
BILKON
Lerd
Groves of Trom
Caves of the Daemons
Forest of Burzee
LAUGHING VALLEY of HOHAHO
Bumpy Man
Turvyland (U)
Maetta
MACVELT
Seventon
JUNKUM
MULGRAVIA
QUOK
THUMBUMBIA
OCEAN
To Pessim's Island
King Anko
Based on the Original Map drawn by Professor H. M. WOGGLEBUG, T.E.
James E. Haff Del.
Dick Martin Sculp.
©1980 by James E. Haff and Dick Martin

List of Chapters

CHAPTER 1

QUEEN CROSS PATCH, the Sixth, stood at her castle window staring crossly down at her cross-patch country. From above it looked like a huge patch-work quilt, spread over the rolling hills of the Winkie Country in Oz. Each of her subjects had a separate cotton-patch, and as each patch produced a different color of cotton and each patch-worker dressed himself and his family in the color of his patch and painted his house the same color too, you can imagine the odd appearance of the Kingdom itself. The Quilties, as the people of Patch were pleased to call themselves, did most of the patch-work in Oz and, as the Kingdoms of Oz are nearly all old-fashioned enough to use and appreciate patch-work quilts, there was plenty of work to be done. Not only did the industrious

Quilties gather the small cotton-patches from their garden patches and stitch them into gay quilts but they did mending and darning as well.

For miles around people brought their old clothes to Queen Cross Patch for repairs, so that Patch was as busy and prosperous a little Kingdom as you would find anywhere, but by no means a pleasant one. Constant picking of the scraps in their garden patches had made the Quilty men exceedingly scrappy, and constant stitching upon the patch-work quilts had made the Quilty ladies extremely cross and crotchety. Indeed, everything about this little country was cross and patchy. All the roads were cross roads, and the houses as patched and shabby as the clothes of the people who lived in them.

But perhaps, of all the Quilties, the Queen, herself, was the crossest and patchiest. She even had a patch over her eye. She had strained it from too much fine sewing. Just now she was straining the other one in an effort to see that all of her subjects were hard at work. Finding that they were, she flounced across the room and sat down at her sewing table. Here, grumbling and scolding to herself, she began sorting patches into separate piles, according to their size and color. Except for her Majesty's mumbles and the occasional snores of a scissor bird, who dozed on a perch by the window, there was not a sound in the great chamber.

But suddenly, with a shrill scream, the Queen flung a handful of patches into the air, toppled off her three-legged throne and went entirely to pieces—extremely small pieces, too.

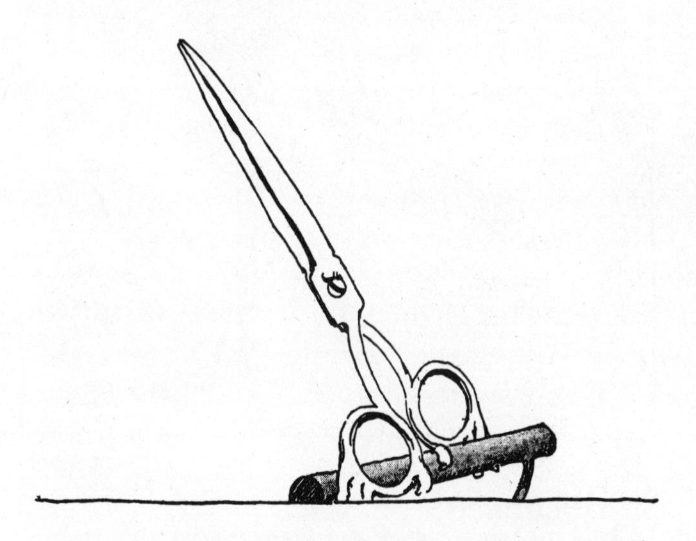

"Help!" shrieked the Scissor Bird, wakening with a bounce. "Help! Help! The Queen has gone to pieces!" At the Scissor Bird's sharp outcries, the Prime Piecer and Chief Scrapper of Patch fairly rushed through the doorway.

"I've been expecting this!" groaned the Prime Piecer, and taking a huge bite from the chunk of beeswax he held in one hand began to chew it gloomily.

"Well, if you've been expecting it you're not surprised," sniffed the Chief Scrapper crossly, "but it's too bad to have it happen at the busiest season of the year. Now we'll have to stop everything and find a new ruler. Hold your bill, Nipper!"

Stamping his foot at the Scissor Bird, the Chief Scrapper of Patch marched stiffly from the room. Neither the Prime Piecer nor the Chief Scrapper seemed to think it queer for the Queen to go to pieces. And no doubt this is because, sooner or later, all of the Quilties do this very thing. Living in a fairy country and being magically constructed they cannot die, so when they wear out, they simply go to pieces. When a Quilty goes to pieces, his relatives or friends sweep up the scraps and put them away in a tidy scrap-bag and in ten years or so he comes out of the bag as good as ever. This does seem a curious custom, but curious or not, that is exactly what happens, and while Scrapper went to fetch the Royal scrap-bag and Piecer the Royal dust-pan, the Scissor Bird flew out of the window to break the news to the patchworking populace.

In a huge sewing circle, the Quilty Dames were stitching upon a quilt and in their separate garden patches, the Quilty men were busily picking cottonpatches. But as the Scissor Bird flew screaming overhead and they realized that Queen Cross Patch had gone to pieces at last, they all stopped working and looked fearfully at one another. Who would be the next ruler of Patch? Whenever a ruler went to pieces another was immediately chosen by the method laid down in the Imperial Scrap Book and always one of the Quilties had been chosen.

Now, curiously enough, no one wanted to be King or Queen, for the ruler of this cross little country had to work six times as hard as anyone else and consequently went to pieces six times faster. Therefore, dropping their thimbles and scissors, the Quilties started to run in every direction, pelting into houses and down cellars, creeping into barrels and hiding themselves behind trees—so that when Piecer and Scrapper issued from the palace not a person was in sight. They had carefully swept up Queen Cross Patch and hung her in a closet, and now, grumbling a little—for choosing a new sovereign was always a troublesome matter—they stepped sternly toward the cotton-wood to the left of the palace. In this wood grew hundreds of spool

cotton-trees—enough, in fact, to furnish all the thread used in the Kingdom. There were pink spool cotton-trees, red spool cotton-trees, green spool cotton-trees, orange spool cotton-trees, and every other color you could imagine. In the center of the little cottonwood grew a somewhat taller tree, bearing always one golden spool. It was to this tree that the Prime Ministers of Patch hurried, for this golden spool was the royal spool of succession, and when cut from the tree led directly to the next ruler of the Kingdom.

Piecer had a large rag-bag over his shoulder, for it was usually necessary to capture a ruler by force; Scrapper had a pair of gold shears and now, standing on tiptoe, he snipped the golden spool from the golden branch and held it expectantly in his hand. There was a regular speech written out in the Royal Scrap Book, and as Scrapper had already chosen three rulers, he knew it by heart.

"Unwind, Oh, Royal Spool of Succession," commanded the little Quilty importantly, "Unwind and lead us to the Imperial Potentate of Patch!" As he came to the word "patch," Scrapper set the spool on the ground and, keeping hold of the golden thread, waited solemnly for something to happen. For a moment the spool lay quietly where he had placed it—then with a little bounce it began to unwind. Letting the gold thread slip through his fingers, Scrapper skipped nimbly after the spool, Piecer following earnestly behind him. Up one cross road and down another rolled the Royal Spool of Succession, past the patched palace, past a dozen patched cottages, on and on and on.

As it passed each cottage, the Quilties within would give a roar of relief, for they knew that for the present the danger of being King or Queen had passed the members of their household. Sometimes the golden spool would roll right into the front door of a cottage and Scrapper and Piecer, thinking their search over, would prepare to seize a sovereign but, just as they did, the spool would whirl out the back door and roll on merrily down the road. But

never before in the history of Patch had it gone so far nor so fast, so that soon the fat Quilty ministers, panting along after it, were completely out of breath and temper. Now the cotton-patches grew thinner and thinner, the little cottages farther and farther apart, and before they half realized it, the golden spool was rolling briskly down a yellow brick highway and the Kingdom of Patch lay far behind them.

"Stop!" grunted Piecer, letting go Scrapper's

coat-tails to which he up to this time had dutifully clung. "Stop! I can go no farther."

"Don't leave me," wailed poor Scrapper, rolling his eyes backward in great distress. Neither of the Quilties had been out of Patch before and the prospect was truly terrifying. Now, whether the magic spool heard the two conversing is hard to tell but, quite suddenly, it stopped and sinking down by the roadway, Piecer and Scrapper began to mop their foreheads with their patched handkerchiefs and fan themselves with their hats.

"Let's go back," quavered Piecer in a low voice.

"But we cannot go back without a ruler," objected Scrapper, who was the bolder of the two. "If we do not find a ruler in four days you very well know that Patch and all of the Quilties will go to pieces. Do you want to go to pieces?" he asked severely.

"No!" said Piecer mournfully, "I don't, but we'll go to pieces anyway, running on at this rate. Something is wrong," puffed the Prime Piecer dolefully. "The spool never took us out of the Kingdom before. It's twisted, I tell you, and dear knows where it will take us."

"It will take us to the next ruler," declared Scrapper, who had recovered some of his breath and most of his courage. "It is our duty to follow. Come!"

"Oh, very well," sighed Piecer, rising to his

feet with a great groan, "but don't blame me if it leads us into a forest and we are torn to bits by bears."

As Piecer finished this cheering speech the thread in Scrapper's hand gave a little pull. The golden spool had started off again. This time, however, it rolled along more slowly and, in spite of their uneasiness, the two Quilties cast interested glances to the right and left. It was all so different from their own patched and shabby little Kingdom. Pleasant yellow cottages and farms dotted the landscape, and the fields and meadows, full of buttercups and daisies, did not look a bit dangerous. On the hill a splendid tin castle shone and glittered in the sun, and though Scrapper and Piecer were quite unaware of it, this was the residence of the Tin Woodman, who ruled over the Land of the East.

Nowhere in Oz is there a more cheerful land than the Country of the Winkies. But just as the two travellers were beginning to enjoy themselves, the spool turned sharply off the highway and plunged down a steep hill. The first jerk flung Scrapper on his face, and as Piecer had hold of his coat-tails he lost his balance too, and over and over they rolled to the bottom.

"Now for the next ruler!" gasped Scrapper. Scrambling to his feet, and without pausing to brush off the dust, he bounded after the spool. It was fairly whistling ahead now, bouncing over rocks and tree stumps, so that the two Patchy Statesmen, in their endeavor to keep up with it, looked like a couple of boys playing leap frog. When it did stop Piecer was too giddy to see, but Scrapper gave a loud roar of anger.

"I don't care what it says," shouted the little Quilty angrily, "I refuse to take orders from a cow. Is this our future sovereign?" he demanded indignantly. The spool had stopped indeed, and under the very horns of a cross brown cow.

"Moo!" bellowed the cow, lowering her head threateningly.

"That's just what we will do," sniffed Scrapper, "move on!" At Scrapper's words, the Spool of Succession, as if it had been waiting for a signal, zipped under the cow, dragging both ministers along, and from the way it behaved in the next half hour, I am convinced that some mighty bad magic had gone into its making. It rushed furiously under fences, over which the breathless Quilties were forced to climb, 'round and 'round trees, till they were almost too dizzy to stand, up hills and down hills, through stickery bushes and over sharp stones. It even dragged them head first into a muddy river.

"Let's go home," blubbered Piecer, shaking himself like a big dog. Fortunately the Quilties could swim, but swimming in quilted trousers and coats was no fun at all and, dripping water and mud, the two sovereign seekers felt more depressed than ever.

"It's bewitched," insisted Piecer, tugging at Scrapper's coat-tails. "Let's go back!"

But Scrapper stubbornly shook his head and trudged stubbornly after the mischievous Spool of Succession. It was unwinding quite deliberately now, but leading them deep into a dangerous looking forest.

"I wish Cross Patch had never gone to pieces," moaned Piecer dismally. "I don't care who's Imperial Potentate. I wish someone else had my position. I wish—"

"There's a sign," interrupted Scrapper. "Look! It says 'Emerald City, thirty-five miles'."

"Emerald City!" panted Piecer, forgetting his weariness for a moment. "Why, that's the capital of Oz. Patches and pincushions! Why, I never expected to see the Emerald City! Maybe our next Queen's in the capital, old fellow!"

"Well, then she ought to make a capital Queen," sighed Scrapper, leaning over to untwine a bramble from his left shin, "but who wants to walk thirty-five miles?"

As he straightened up, the gold spool whirled between two tall trees and came to a complete standstill on a short foot-path. A rustic railing ran along the edge of the path and, taking hold of the railing, Scrapper began looking anxiously around for the future ruler of Patch.

"Do you see anything?" he queried, looking over his shoulder.

"No, but I feel something," grunted Piecer,

peering anxiously down at his feet. "Beeswax and basting threads!"

Next instant both Quilties leapt into the air. Then, taking a firmer hold upon the railing and on each other, they clung desperately together, for the foot-path, rising up on its hundred broad feet, was rushing like the wind through the gloomy forest.

"Are—we—going—to—pieces?" shouted the Prime Piecer, not daring to open his eyes.

Cautiously Scrapper opened one eye and the first thing that met his gaze was a neat notice tacked on the rustic railing. It was only a blur, so fast were they travelling, but opening the other eye he managed to decipher it.

"This foot-path runs straight to the Emerald

City. Hold tight. No stamping or kicking allowed.

"Private Property of the Wizard of Oz."

"Well, hurrah!" exclaimed Scrapper, thumping his companion on the chest. "We're not going to pieces, we're going to the Emerald City! Going! Going! Why, here we are!"

And they were too. Right at the gates of the loveliest city in Oz. The foot-path, having accomplished its journey in less than a minute, now tilted its passengers rudely off and, coiling up like a serpent, went to sleep under a lime drop tree. Too overcome to do anything but blink at the gleaming spires and turrets of the capital, the two simple Quilties stood stunned and still. But a business-like tug from the gold thread brought them out of their trance.

The Spool of Succession had slid off the path with them and was now rolling gaily through the gates of the city. Holding fast to one another, and scarcely daring to breathe, the fat little ministers of Patch went tiptoeing after the golden spool.

The New Queen of the Quilties

CHAPTER 2

THE EMERALD CITY, which Scrapper and Piecer were now entering, is the capital of Oz and lies in the exact center of that merry and magical Kingdom. Oz, as many of you know, is a funny and fascinating fairyland, oblong in shape and surrounded, for protection, by a deadly desert of sand. There are four large countries in Oz; the yellow Winkie Land of the East, the purple Gillikin country of the North, the blue Munchkin country of the West and the red lands of the Quadlings in the South. Each of these four countries is divided into many smaller countries of which Patch is the seven hundred and fifth, but all are subject to one ruler and governed by laws laid down by the Queen of the realm.

The rulers of Oz always lived in the capital, not only because it is so central and convenient, but because it is the most beautiful and enchanting city in the whole fairy world. Its cottages and castle fairly twinkle with emeralds and these precious stones, studding the walls and even the marble walks, give the air a soft glow and shimmer, making gardens greener, fountains more sparkling and everything more glittering and gay.

Ozma, a little girl fairy, is the present ruler of Oz and the wisest and gentlest sovereign the fairy country has ever known. With her in the Emerald City live fifty seven thousand, three hundred and eighteen gay Ozites and nearly a hundred celebrities, for Ozma has invited to her court the most interesting characters from her four fairy kingdoms.

The Scarecrow, a lively fellow stuffed with straw, is perhaps the most famous. He has a palace of his own, but is a frequent visitor at the capital. Then there is the Tin Woodman, who rules over the Winkies and is a splendidly polished gentleman of tin, and Sir Hokus of Pokes, a knight seven centuries old, Jack Pumpkinhead, a singular person carved from wood with a large pumpkin for a head, Tik Tok, a machine man who winds up like a clock and does everything but live, the famous Wizard of Oz and so many more that twenty histories have already been written about their queer doings.

On this late afternoon, as the two bewildered Quilties trod timidly down the streets of the capital, Ozma was busily conferring with

Princess Dorothy about curtains. Dorothy is a little Kansas girl, who was blown to Oz in a cyclone and later was made a Princess and invited to live in the palace. She is Ozma's favorite adviser and not only helps her rule over the turbulent tribes of Oz, but is consulted about everything, even such small matters as new ribbons for the palace pets or, as now, about castle curtains. Choosing curtains is fun and there were so many colors and fabrics, it took the two girls quite a long time to decide. They had about settled on green taffeta, edged with gold fringe, when a terrified cry came echoing in from the garden.

"What was that?" cried Dorothy, and dropping a roll of taffeta, she rushed to the window. Ozma followed quickly and, in some alarm, the two stared down over the flowered slopes and green terraces. But not a soul was in sight and after waiting for another scream, they concluded that the first was the shout of some mischievous boy and gaily returned to their curtains. Had they looked five minutes sooner, they would have been surprised indeed. Five minutes before Scrapper and Piecer, toiling breathlessly after the Spool of Succession, had run straight into the palace garden. Darting here and there, it had led them to a secluded grape arbor. On a green bench under the arbor sat a most amazing young lady, and as the two Quilties stared at her in perfect astonishment and admiration the golden spool stopped at her feet.

It was the Patchwork Girl, one of the very jolliest of Ozma's subjects. She had been made originally by a wizard's wife out of an old crazy quilt and neatly stuffed with cotton. Her eyes were silver suspender buttons, her tongue a piece of red velvet and her hair a bunch of yarn that refused to stay down. Margolotte, the

wizard's wife, had intended Scraps for a servant, but when the wizard mixed up her brains a double portion of fun and cleverness had got in by mistake. When he brought her to life, Scraps refused to work and ran off to the Emerald City where she has lived ever since, making life lively for everyone and having more fun herself than a cageful of monkeys. Being constructed from a crazy quilt makes her exceedingly reckless and gay and as more than half her conversation is in verse, Scraps is a most amusing and delightful companion. To the weary and already homesick Quilties she seemed a vision of perfect loveliness.

"Superb!" gloated Piecer, throwing both arms round Scrapper's neck in his excitement.

"A beauty!" exulted Scrapper, returning Piecer's embrace with interest. Indeed, so delighted were they at the appearance of their future sovereign that they began to dance up and down and fairly hug one another for joy. A sharp exclamation from the Patchwork Girl made them stop.

"Ragmen apply at the rear!" cried Scraps, pointing imperiously toward the back of the castle.

"Ragmen!" The Quilties exchanged indignant glances. The spool had led them such a chase that their clothes were torn and dusty and the bag over Piecer's shoulder added a convincing touch to the picture. No wonder Scraps thought them ragmen. Piecer was about to explain, but

Scrapper, afraid that this bewitching damsel might escape them, rushed forward impetuously and seized her hand.

"Scat!" screamed the Patchwork Girl, snatching it angrily away. "What do you take me for?"

"Because we have to," confided the Chief Scrapper mysteriously. "We take you for what you are, a Queen. Three cheers for the Queen of the Quilties!" wheezed Scrapper, signaling slyly to Piecer. And while the Patchwork Girl fell back, stiff with astonishment, Piecer clapped the bag over her head. Then together

the two little Quilties shook her down into the bottom and pulled the string tight. It was the frightened scream of Scraps, as she disappeared into the rag bag that Dorothy and Ozma had heard, but by the time they reached the window, she was out of the garden. Thrusting a sharp stick through the neck of the sack, the Ministers of Patch hoisted it to their shoulders and, with the bag itself swinging violently between them, started on a run for the gates. They would never have succeeded in kidnapping Scraps nor escaping unobserved had it not been for the foot-path. After a short nap it had grown curious about the two strangers it had brought to the city and pattering into the royal garden began to search for them. Usually the Wizard

of Oz kept this mischievous piece of property tied up when not in use, but today he had forgotten to do so and, enjoying its holiday, the little foot-path was running perfectly wild. Coming upon Piecer and Scrapper as they dashed headlong over flower beds and borders, it scooped them neatly up and by a short, little known route carried them straight out of the Emerald City.

For a time the Quilties were too shocked to realize what had happened. Then Scrapper, shaken out of his stupor by a terrible jolt as the foot-path jumped over a boulder, gasped weakly. "Why, it's the same flying path that brought us to the capital!"

"Yes, but where is it flying now?" wailed Piecer, tightening his hold upon the rag bag. Inside Scraps was thrashing around in a frantic effort to escape, her screams and threats somewhat muffled by the collection of pieces already in the bag. "Can't we steer it?" panted the Prime Piecer wildly, "or stop it or something?" Scrapper shook his head violently, then catching sight of a green card tacked on the rustic railing fairly pounced upon it.

"Write directions here," advised the card. There was a pencil attached to the railing by a long cord, so Scrapper seized the pencil and wrote hastily, "Take us to the Kingdom of Patch."

The foot-path jiggled so frightfully while he wrote 'tis a wonder it could understand the directions as all, but as he let the pencil drop, it turned sharply in its tracks and started racing in the opposite direction, tripping and stumbling in its eagerness to get ahead. By the time they reached the Quilty Kingdom, the three travellers were so shaken up and down they tumbled off the path in a perfect heap of exhaustion. Even Scraps, in her imprisoning bag, had nothing at all to say. Not satisfied with shaking them nearly to bits, the foot-path gave Piecer a playful kick with its forty-ninth foot and then, jumping over a green cotton patch, gaily took its departure. Now, ever since morning, the Patch-workers had been anxiously awaiting the return of their ministers and, as the two exhausted sovereign seekers rolled through the gates, a great crowd of Quilties came hurrying to meet them.

"What have you bagged? Who is our ruler? Show us the Imperial Potentate," they cried, clattering their shears and shaking their sewing boxes. Seeing that nothing would satisfy them but an immediate sight of the Queen, Scrapper scrambled wearily to his feet and began fumbling with the strings of the bag.

"Will your Imperial Highness deign to step out?" suggested Scrapper, sticking his head cautiously into the bag.

"Out!" shrilled Scraps, and bouncing up like a Jill in the box, gave Scrapper a resounding smack on the ear.

"You villain ragman
Take me back.
How dare you hurl
Me in a sack?"

she cried furiously and, whirling upon Piecer, boxed his ears as soundly as she had boxed Scrapper's. At this the delight of the Quilties knew no bounds. They began to cheer and stamp with approval.

"What a fine temper! What a marvelous beauty! She's the Queen for us." And raising their shears they shouted altogether, "Hurrah for the Queen of the Quilties!"

"Try to act like a Queen, can't you?" puffed Scrapper, seizing the agitated Patchwork Girl by the arm.

"You're making a great hit!" whispered Piecer persuasively. "Give me your name, maiden, so I can announce it to your subjects." By this time Scraps had recovered enough to look around and what she saw interested her greatly. The gaudy Quilty Kingdom, with its gay cotton patches, the Quilties themselves, in their oddly patched clothes, seemed as beautiful to Scraps as she seemed to them.

"What do you mean? Am I a Queen?" she demanded, rolling her suspender button eyes from side to side. The Prime Ministers of Patch nodded and, as they did, two Quilties, with a huge patchwork arm chair on wheels, pushed their way through the crowd.

"Quick, now, your name," begged Piecer. When Scraps, in an excited whisper, imparted the information, he cried in a loud voice: "Hats off to Her Patchesty! Three cheers for Queen Scraps of Patch!"

The cheers were given with a will and, as Piecer grandly handed the Patchwork Girl into the royal rolling chair, the excited Quilties

fairly pelted her with patches, tomato pin-cushions and hard spools of cotton. Luckily Scraps is a stuffed person, with no feeling at

all, otherwise she might have been hurt by these flying missiles. As it was, she sat back grandly, bowing now to the left, now to the right and feeling more important than she had ever felt in her whole cotton career. When they reached the patched palace, two Quilty boys were waiting on the steps, one with the coronet and the other with the crown jewels and, amid the further cheers of the populace, Scraps was crowned Queen of the Kingdom and led triumphantly into her castle. The crown was a round sewing basket, the crown jewels a string of old spools, but scarcely noticing the odd character of her royal regalia, Scraps strutted proudly up and down the shabby hall of the palace, rehearsing grand speeches and queenly gestures. As for Scrapper and Piecer—too weary to bother about supper or bed—they immediately locked all the windows and doors and fell into a heavy slumber on a hall bench.

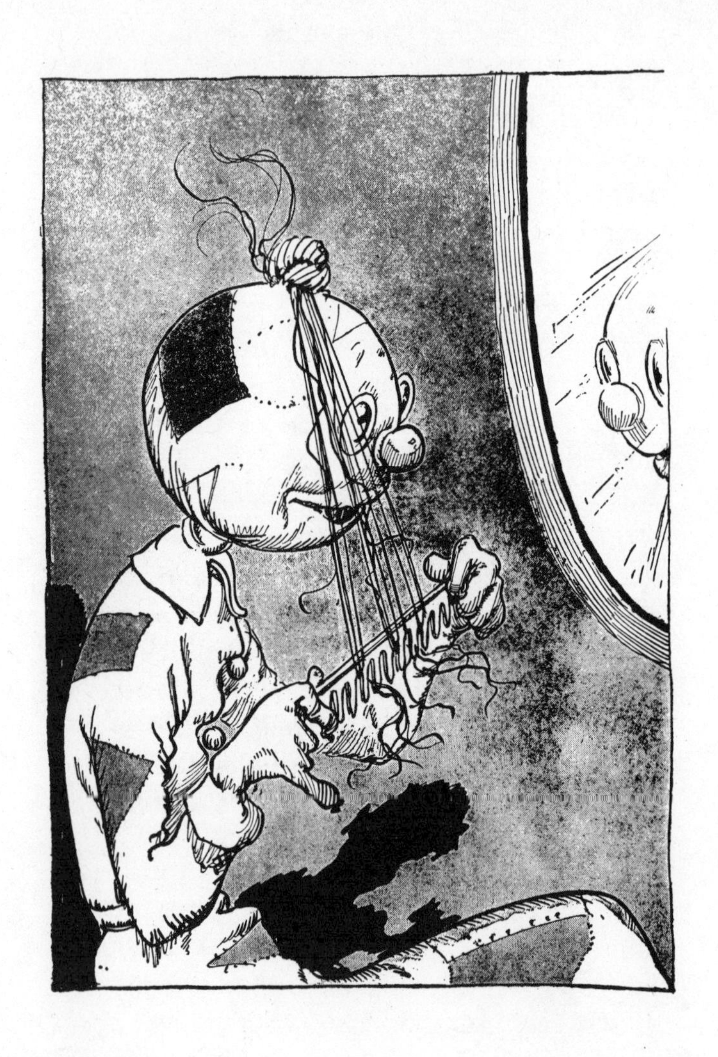

CHAPTER 3

HUNGRY from their long fast, for they had eaten nothing the day before, and wearied by their long quest, the two Quilty statesmen arose early next morning. "High time to instruct her Highness in the duties of her office," yawned Scrapper, ruffling up his hair.

"I hope she has breakfast ready," muttered Piecer, groaning a little as he straightened his knees and stretched out his arms. "And I hope this Queen lasts a long time, Scrapper, for another day like yesterday would be the end of me. Come on, let's see what she's doing."

Not requiring any sleep, Scraps had spent the first half of the night wondering how she had come to be Queen. Then, giving it up, she spent the other half dancing and singing and composing long speeches to deliver to her subjects. As Piecer and Scrapper stepped into the main hall of the palace, she was arranging her yarn hair before a long mirror. Catching sight of them in the glass, she spun gaily round and clapping her crown on sideways cried haughtily:

"Vassals, fetch my rolling chair.
Your Queen desires to take the air!"

"Stuff and Nonsense!" sputtered Scrapper, amazed at the Patchwork Girl's audacious verse. "Don't you know the coronation is over and it's time to get to work?"

"Work?" shrilled Scraps, catching hold of a patched portiere to steady herself. "Queens are not supposed to work. Where are the servants?"

"There are no servants," answered Scrapper calmly. "The Queen does all the work here. Just read off the list of her Majesty's duties, Piecer, old fellow."

Putting on his specs, Piecer drew a long sheet of paper from his patched pocket and began: "The Queen of Patch, on arising, shall prepare the breakfast of her two chief advisers (meaning us)," explained Piecer, looking severely at the Patchwork Girl over his spectacles. "She shall make the beds," he continued complacently, his voice growing higher with each item, "sweep the floors, dust the furniture, scrub the steps, wash the windows, sort the patches, count the cotton spools, separate the old clothes for mending, feed the Scissor Bird, help pick tomato pin-cushions, scold the Patchworkers—and—"

"Stop!" commanded Scraps, flinging up her arm imperiously.

"But I'm not nearly finished," objected Piecer, rattling the paper impatiently.

"Well, I am!" The Patchwork Girl's suspender buttons glittered angrily behind the steel spectacles. "Get someone else to be your sovereign," she cried. "You don't want a Queen, you want a cook, a housekeeper and a Grandma!" Snatching the work basket from her head, she dashed it to the floor and jumping on it with both feet shouted defiantly:

"Eeejee, weejee, squeejee, squb!
I will not sweep, I will not scrub!
I will not scrub! I will not dust!
So let those dust and scrub who must!"

"Better save your strength for your work," advised Piecer, stepping back a few paces. "You're Chief Scrapper," he whispered hurriedly to his companion. "You settle her while I fetch the Scissor Bird."

As the door slammed upon Piecer, the Chief Scrapper faced the Patchwork Girl. "Go on, get as mad as you please," he urged cheerfully. "The madder you are the better we like you. The crosser you grow the better queen you'll make for Patch, our Queens must be good scolders," he chuckled, rubbing his hands gleefully together.

"I'm not your queen," screamed Scraps, stamping one foot and then the other. "Take me back to the Emerald City, you miserable ragamuffin. I am a free subject of Ozma of Oz."

"Oh, no! You're Queen of Patch, now," corrected Scrapper, picking up the waste basket and jamming it down upon her cotton forehead. "You were chosen by the royal Spool of Succession to be our ruler!"

While Scraps listened in amazement, he explained how the former queen had gone to pieces and how the golden spool had led them to the Emerald City.

"And you think, just because your silly spool tagged me, that I'm going to stay and do all your work?" exclaimed Scraps, snapping her cotton fingers under Scrapper's nose. "Kazupp-kazick, you make me sick!" Rushing to the door, she jerked it open, bumped against Piecer, on his way in, and sat down with a thud.

"What a pretty creature," chirped the Scissor Bird, who had flown over Piecer's head. "Is this the new Queen?"

Scrapper nodded.

"She knows almost as many cross words as the last one," he chuckled admiringly. "But she refuses to work."

"Oh, I think she'll work now," smiled Piecer. With a significant wink at his companion, he thrust a broom into Scrap's hands and, turning to the Scissor Bird, said quietly: "If her Majesty refuses to clean the castle, just cut off her head!"

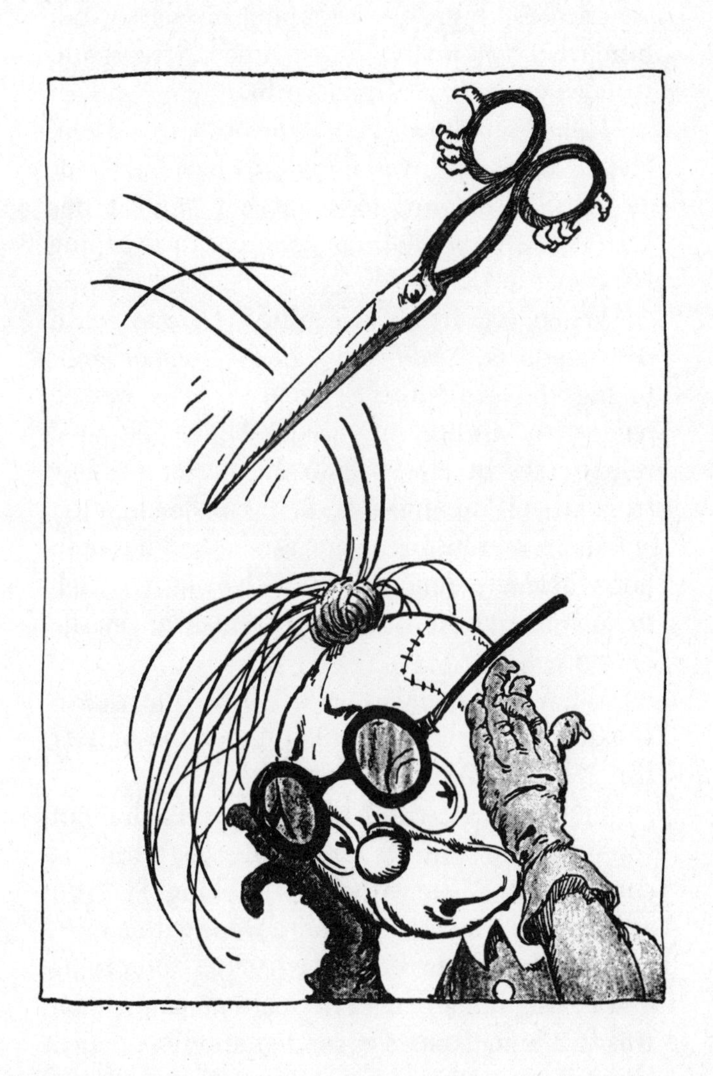

"Nothing would give me more pleasure," chortled the bird, and snapping his scissor bill hungrily, he swooped down upon Scraps and snipped an inch off her yarn hair.

"Help!" screamed the Patchwork Girl. "Help! Help!" But there was no one to help her and, as the Scissor Bird took another snip at her yarn, she seized the broom and fell to sweeping for dear life.

"When you finish sweeping, you may wash the windows," said the Chief Scrapper and, taking the arm of the Prime Piecer, passed pompously out into the garden. All day, pursued relentlessly by the Scissor Bird, Scraps flew from one task to another. Being made of cotton she did not grow tired, but as she had never in her whole life done anything she did not wish to do, you can imagine how furiously angry she became.

"Wait till Ozma hears of this!" she raged, shaking her scrubbing brush under the Scissor Bird's bill. "Just wait!"

"I'll wait!" yawned the Scissor Bird, "but you'll have to wait too, and while we're waiting suppose you go on with the scrubbing."

Poor Scraps, she could have wept with anger, but she had not been constructed for crying and having not a tear in her cotton constitution was forced to express her indignation in groans, shouts and threatening verses. To these the Scissor Bird paid no attention whatsoever and by night-fall Scraps had not even energy enough to make verses. After complaining bitterly about their dinner, and it must be confessed that Scraps, having had no experience, proved a poor cook, the two Quiltie Ministers locked her securely in the palace sitting-room and went off to tell their fellow townsmen about the Emerald City. They took the Scissor Bird with them and, left to her own devices at last, the Patchwork Girl sank into a broken chair and began to rock to and fro.

"No wonder the Queens go to pieces so fast," groaned Scraps, anxiously examining a rip in her cotton finger. She had caught it on a nail while scrubbing the castle steps.

"Kazupp Kazoo, what shall I do?
Stay here and go to pieces, too? Never!"

Springing up, she took the candle the Quilties had placed on the center table and ran from one window to the other. But the windows were all locked and barred and, after rattling the door knobs and pounding on the wall, she sat dejectedly down in the rocking chair again. There was nothing in the room to amuse her. All the books in the bookcase were needle-books, all the cushioins were pin-cushions and the wall was simply covered with cross stitched mottoes.

"A stitch in time saves nine!" sniffed Scraps, scornfully reading the one nearest her. "Well, who wants to save nine? Why should nine be saved any more than six or seven?"

There was no one to argue it with, so after a little silence she murmured: "I wonder what's in that chest?" Except for a few rickety chairs and the sewing-table, the chest was the only other piece of furniture in the room. Taking the candle, Scraps walked over to the chest, and dropping on her knees, cautiously lifted the lid. At first she thought it was empty, but, as three or four drops of hot candle grease dripped inside, a low growl rumbled out of the darkness. In some alarm Scraps jumped back.

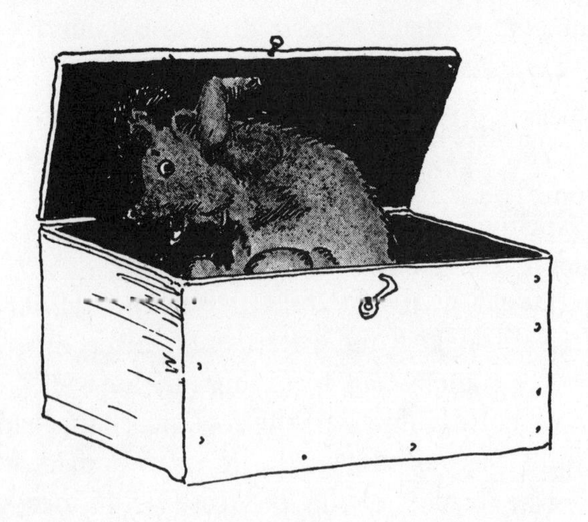

"Go away!" roared a gruff voice. "Do your own scolding, I'm sleepy! Shut that lid, I tell you!"

"Shut it yourself!" cried the Patchwork Girl, who was extremely tired of being ordered about. Besides she was a little frightened. At this, there was a short pause, followed by a surprised grunt, and presently a rumpled head appeared above the edge of the chest. It was a small brown bear. Blinking at Scraps, it grumbled crossly, "Where's the Queen? Who in scratch are you?"

"I'm the Queen, who in Patch are you?" answered the Patchwork Girl saucily. The bear regarded her attentively for some time before he answered. Then putting his head on one side he explained calmly, "Why, I'm a pet of the late Queen Cross Patch. Has she gone to pieces?"

Scraps nodded. "I don't see why she wanted a bear for a pet," she added frankly.

"You look bright, but I'm afraid you're quite dumb," sniffed the bear, climbing out of the chest. "Why shouldn't she have a bear for a pet? Isn't a bear about the crossest pet one could find? I helped Cross Patch with the grumbling and growling when she was tired. I'll help you if you wish, though it will be a little harder. Just looking at you makes me want to laugh."

"Well, why don't you?" asked Scraps, seating herself in the rocker again.

"Sh—hh! Do you want me to lose my position?" breathed the little bear, looking around anxiously. "I mustn't laugh. Don't you know a bear is supposed to be cross? You have to be pretty cross to keep your place in this country!"

"Well, I don't intend to stay in this country," announced Scraps, rocking vigorously backward and forward. "I was kidnapped and crowned Queen against my will and I intend to run away as soon as I can. Princess Ozma may send for me any minute, too. All she has to do is to look in the Magic Picture." This was quite true, for in Ozma's palace hangs an enchanted picture, showing a country landscape. If the little fairy ruler wishes to locate any of her subjects, she has but to command them to appear and the Magic Picture immediately shows where they are and what they are doing. All of this, and a bit about Ozma and the Emerald City, Scraps explained to the cross little bear and he listened most earnestly, wiggling his buttony nose with interest.

"What's your name?" asked Scraps presently.

"Grumpy!" answered the bear gruffly. "What's yours?"

"Scraps!" said the Patchwork Girl, kicking her heels against the rocker.

Now, one of the delightful things about Oz is that all the animals and birds can talk; and as talk of any kind interested Scraps she began to feel quite cheerful and like herself.

"You mean Queen Scraps," corrected the little bear, eyeing the work-basket on her head with great respect.

"Not if I can help it!" cried the Patchwork Girl, springing out of her seat and rattling the crown jewels defiantly. "The country is all right, but who ever heard of a Queen doing all the work? It's ridiculous."

"Queen Cross Patch liked to work," muttered Grumpy. Then, sitting down thoughtlessly on a pin-cushion, he arose with a loud roar.

"Well, I don't," said Scraps, while Grumpy, growling furiously, pulled two needles from his fur. "So I hope Ozma looks in the Magic Picture soon, but whether she does or not I shall run off first chance I get—

"Back to the city of sun and song,
Back to the city where I belong!"

"It'll be a long time before they let you," observed Grumpy thoughtfully, "and if you try to escape the Scissor Bird will cut off your head. What would you do then?"

"Have it sewed on again," declared Scraps stoutly, but she shivered a little at the prospect and in a slightly shaky voice inquired, "Don't you know any games or riddles? No one's around now and we might as well have some fun."

Grumpy shook his head, then brightening up a little he slid out of his chair. "Cross Patch and I always cuffed each other a bit after dinner," he said casually.

"Cuffed each other!" gasped Scraps. "What for?"

"For practice," explained Grumpy solemnly. "You have no idea how many new cross words we learned that way. It's simply astonishing what cross words you can think of when someone thumps you on the ear. Come on—let's try it. You'll need to know a lot of cross words." Drawing back his fuzzy arm, Grumpy gave the Patchwork Girl a cuff that sent her flying into the corner.

"What a pleasant pastime!" puffed Scraps, picking herself up with a flounce. "Do you call that fun?" she demanded, shaking the dust scornfully out of her skirts.

"Well, what do you want to do then?" mumbled the little bear sullenly. "That's the only game I know. Say, someone's at the door! Listen!"

Someone certainly was. First, the bell rang long and clangingly. Then came such a series of thumps, kicks and slams that all the cross stitched mottoes fell sideways.

"Oh!" shrilled the Patchwork Girl, flinging

up her arms joyously, "I know. Ozma has sent someone to rescue me. Come on Grumpy, we'll let them in."

"How do you know it's rescuers?" shivered the little bear anxiously. "They sound like robbers to me!"

"Get out!" cried Scraps, running over to the door.

"We can't get out," Grumpy reminded her patiently, "for we're locked in good and tight."

"That's so," sighed the Patchwork Girl, pressing her cotton nose to the window bars. "They'll have to break down the door."

"Sounds as if they had," sputtered the little bear, as a terrible crash sounded from the hallway. "Here they come!" Jumping head first into the chest Grumpy pulled down the lid.

Peter Flies with an Odd Bird

CHAPTER 4

"NOTHING at all ever happens here," exclaimed Peter, digging his hands deep into his pockets and staring discontentedly out of the window.

"There's a balloon man on the corner," chuckled his grandfather, who was standing just behind Peter. "Go buy yourself a balloon." With another chuckle he dropped a quarter into Peter's hand and went back to his evening paper.

"I'm too old for balloons," said Peter with great disgust. "I should think you'd know that, grandfather."

"Then buy me one," laughed the old gentleman, winking provokingly. There was no use arguing with a person like that, so Peter, fully intending to buy some marbles and a double nut sundae, ran out of the house.

Peter's home was in Philadelphia, facing on a large public square and the balloon man, his boisterous wares nearly tugging him off his feet, stood on the corner nearest Peter. There was something mysterious about the man. His face was dark and merry and his long pointed beard and slouch hat gave him the appearance of a merchant from some far country, so that in spite of himself Peter stopped.

"A balloon, young gentleman?" inquired the dealer, bowing politely to the little boy. "What do you say to this one?" Separating a bright green one from the bunch, he held it out invitingly.

"How much?" asked Peter doubtfully. He liked being called a young gentleman, and the more he looked at the green balloon, the more it fascinated him. The balloon man had already seen the quarter in Peter's hand and quickly stating that twenty-five cents was the price, he thrust the balloon upon Peter and pocketed his quarter, all so quickly the little boy fairly gasped. Why, he had not even made up his mind to buy, and yet here he was with the green balloon and there was the man with his quarter. Uncertainly, Peter stood staring at the balloon man.

"It's a bird!" whispered the merchant, leaning forward to touch the balloon lovingly with the tips of his fingers. "Ah-h-h!" As the balloon man said "Ah!" a crowd of Peter's friends turned the corner and not wishing them to catch him with anything so babyish as a balloon, Peter started to run across the square. And never had Peter run so easily. Each step took him four or five paces ahead, and when he found himself bounding entirely over the fountain in the center of the square, he wisely decided to stop running. So he did, but it made no difference. His legs stopped moving, to be sure, but Peter himself shot upward, soaring lightly as a feather over tree tops, house tops, huge buildings and church steeples. Not until the tall figure of William Penn, on the Town Hall, faded into the merest dot, did Peter remember the balloon man's words.

"Why, it *is* a bird," murmured the startled boy, blinking at the comical creature above him. The stem of the balloon to which he clung had turned to a strong stiff leg, while the balloon itself had expanded into a plump, green balloon bird. It careened through the air without any motion of wings or body and for a while, Peter, hanging to its leg, was too frightened to open his mouth. The city had disappeared long ago and, as they pushed up toward the clouds, Peter, regaining a little of his courage, gave the bird's leg a sharp pull. "Stop!" shouted Peter in as commanding a voice as he could muster.

"Stop yourself," retorted the balloon bird sharply, and the words came in tiny explosions like the pop pop of an air gun. "Do you think I enjoy having my leg pulled?" it chirped indignantly.

"But where are we going?" cried Peter anxiously.

"Balloon Island!" popped the bird, bending its head to get a better view of the little boy. "Hold tight, for if you let go, you'll probably puncture yourself on a steeple."

Peter had been thinking this very thing himself. "You are a present to Queen Luna from Sandaroo," continued the bird calmly. "She needed an airrend boy, so Sandaroo sent you."

"The balloon man?" gasped Peter, scarcely believing his ears.

"He's not a balloon man," replied the bird disdainfully. "He's Lord High Bouncer of Balloona. You were picked for airrend boy," he continued placidly, "because you look strong and stout and because the balloon boys on the island are always puncturing themselves or exploding. Did you ever explode?" asked the bird severely.

"People don't explode," answered the little boy scornfully, "and I'm not going to be an errand boy for a lot of balloonatics either," he shouted angrily. "You'd better let me go or I'll tell my grandfather on you."

"Let go if you want to," said the bird carelessly. "You're holding on to me, aren't you?" This was only too true, and after one dizzy look downward, Peter tightened his clutch on the balloon bird's leg and wondered desperately what to do. "You must tread lightly when we land on the island," warned the balloon bird, after a short silence, during which they covered miles of air, "but I daresay it will be all right after you are blown up."

"Blown up," coughed Peter, "why, what do you mean?"

"Well, you wouldn't do as you are," murmured the bird, rolling its eyes disapprovingly down at the little boy, "so the Queen has a splendid plan. She will cut a tiny hole in your back and then have you blown up till you can float as easily as we do. Oh, you'll enjoy floating," promised the balloon bird, diving through a moist cloud bank.

Peter doubted that he would enjoy floating, he doubted it very much, and the more he thought about being blown up and the hole that was to be cut in his back the more

dreadfully uneasy he became. His arms ached from the long swing through the air and, as the balloon bird plunged through a particularly black cloud, Peter took a long breath and let go.

"Maybe . . . I'll land . . . on . . . something . . . soft!" panted Peter, as he turned over and over and then dropped straight downward. "Anyway, it won't be any worse than being cut and blown up." He had fallen several miles by this time and it was so confusing, tumbling through clouds and air-ways, and the wind made such a frightful whistling in his ears, he finally gave up thinking altogether and closed his eyes.

Splash! With a terrific slap, Peter struck the surface of a shining blue ocean, the force of his fall carrying him to the very bottom, where he bumped his head severely on a clam shell. Dazed and choking, Peter rose to the surface and almost mechanically began to swim. After several strokes, he shook the water from his eyes and looked around him. Then he gave a little exclamation of excitement and relief. Not more than twenty paces off lay a small, straggly looking island.

"Well, this is better than being blown up," gulped Peter, heading straight for the island. "Maybe some fishermen live here and maybe some boats pass. Gee whillikens, won't grandfather be surprised when he hears about this, though!"

Immensely cheered, Peter cut swiftly through the choppy blue waves, and the water was soon shallow enough for him to wade ashore. The island was not much larger than the public square at home. A few sea gulls circled aimlessly overhead, but so far as Peter could see there were no people or houses. First he walked completely round the island, then, feeling rather depressed, started across. The soil was poor and rocky and there were only about a dozen trees altogether. When he had come to the top

of a small hill, Peter sank down on a heap of rocks and began to wring the water from his coat. How long he sat there wondering what he should eat, how he should endure the loneliness or ever find his way back to Philadelphia, Peter never knew. But he suddenly became aware of a rattle and rumble below and out from the opposite side of the rock heap sprang a perfectly furious little man. He was gray as the rocks himself, and his long, wispy white hair and beard blew and snapped in the wind.

"Get off my chimney, idiot!" screamed the old gentleman, dancing wrathfully up and down. "Can't you see you're filling my cave with smoke?"

Stopping right in the middle of his dance, he glared long and searchingly at the little boy. Then, bursting into loud sobs, he began to hop 'round and 'round on one leg, wiping his tears on his whiskers and fairly sizzling with indignation.

"To think!" he shouted, raising his arms to the heavens, "To think, that after five years of loneliness a miserable mortal should fall on this island! Why couldn't it have been a gnome or a witch or somebody real and interesting? I hate children," shrieked the angry little fellow, stamping his curly foot at Peter.

Peter had been so startled by the sudden appearance of the old gentleman and then so surprised at his curious actions that he had said nothing at all. But now he jumped angrily off the rock heap. He's no bigger than I am, thought Peter courageously, and he needn't think he can talk to me like that. "Is this your island?" he asked stiffly.

"Of course it's my island!" spluttered the little man. "Go away, I hate children."

"Well, I can't help that," answered Peter. "Besides, I'm not a child. I'm nine years old and in the Fifth-B."

"I don't care what you're in," shrilled the little islander. "You're in my way now, and if I had my magic belt I'd turn you to a potato and mash you for supper. Don't you know I'm a King?" he squealed, thumping himself three times upon the chest.

"Well, you don't act like one," answered Peter, in disgust. "If you are the King of this island I wish you'd give me some supper and a place to sleep."

"King of this island!" screamed the angry little man. "I'm Ruggedo, the Rough, the one and only Metal Monarch and ruler over five hundred thousand gnomes besides."

"Gnomes!" murmured Peter, pushing back his cap. He had read about these underground elves, who mine all the precious stones in and out of the world, but he had never really believed in them.

"Yes, gnomes!" boasted the little gray gentleman, marching proudly up and down.

"Where are they?" inquired Peter, a little anxiously. For, thought Peter to himself, if they are all as cross and tempery as this one, life on the island is going to be very unpleasant and dangerous.

"You stand there and ask me that," howled the Gnome King furiously. "Don't you know I've been banished from my Kingdom for years and made a prisoner on this ridiculous little island, just because I tried to get back my magic belt from Ozma of Oz? Don't you know it was a miserable child who stole it in the first place. I hate children," repeated the Gnome King, clutching his hair with both hands and snapping his wicked little eyes at Peter.

"If you've been here all that time by yourself I should think you'd be glad to have someone to talk to," ventured the little boy, seating himself carefully on a rock. "I read a book about Oz once," he went on in an interested voice, "but I didn't know it was really true. Is Ozma still Queen and does Dorothy still live in the Emerald City?"

"Dorothy's the girl who stole my belt," sputtered Ruggedo, for it was the Gnome King. "If you have read about Dorothy, you must know about me."

"You weren't in the book I read," explained Peter patiently, "but if you know Dorothy and Ozma, they must be real and if we are near Oz, maybe you can tell me how to get there?"

"If I knew do you suppose I'd be here?" yelled Ruggedo. Picking up a rock, he flung it at Peter's head and rushed violently into his cavern. Peter dodged the rock and, almost wishing he had stuck with the balloon bird, stared dejectedly out to sea. The sun was sinking in the west and the prospect of a long stay on the barren island with the dreadful little Gnome King was not at all cheering.

"I'll probably starve to death," sighed Peter,

kicking gloomily at a stone. Then, remembering some string in his pocket, he pulled it out and, fastening a small piece of wire on the string, started toward the beach with the intention of catching a few fish for his dinner. Halfway there, he came to a small sluggish stream and, casting his line into its muddy waters, sat down to wait for a bite. He had no matches but thought maybe if he caught a few fish and offered Ruggedo one he might allow him to cook over his fire.

Now Ruggedo had fully intended to stay in his cave and not speak another word to Peter, but finally his curiosity got the best of him. After you have been all alone for five years, even a creature you despise is better than no one at all, so presently he came stalking out again. Peter had in the meantime decided to be as polite as possible to the old gnome, for no one could help him. Therefore, as Ruggedo approached, puffing away at a short clay pipe, he waved to him quite cheerfully.

"Don't wave at me," wheezed Ruggedo, taking his pipe out of his mouth and frowning darkly. "I'm a King, I am!"

"Oh, what difference does that make?" said Peter impatiently. "We're both stranded, aren't we? Let's stop quarreling and try to find a way off the island. Don't boats ever stop here and how far away is this land of Oz, anyway?"

"Boats!" scoffed the Gnome King, "I've been here five years and not one boat has passed. As for Oz, you are in the very middle of the Nonestic Ocean and about as far from Oz as you could possibly be."

"You mean to say you've been here five years?" gasped Peter incredulously, "and nothing has happened in all that time?"

"Nothing—but you," answered the Gnome King.

"Well, you needn't think I'm going to stay that long," blustered Peter, jerking at his fish line in great agitation. "I'll build a boat, or a raft or something."

Taking his pipe from his mouth, the old gnome looked at Peter almost respectfully. He

had often thought of building a raft himself but, being a King and naturally quite unskillful and lazy, he had never really gotten down to it.

"If you help me off this island," he puffed

after a short pause, "I'll make you the richest boy in the world."

"Humph!" grunted Peter, not much impressed by the old gnome's promises. Just then, his line gave a tug and he was pulling it up quite joyfully when Ruggedo seized his arm.

"Look!" shuddered the gnome, pointing a trembling finger out to sea. Not far from the island, the waters of the Nonestic Ocean were boiling and churning in a terrifying manner. As Peter jumped to his feet, the waves arose in a mighty green wall and, with a deafening roar, came crashing downward.

CHAPTER 5

FLUNG flat upon their faces by the terrific shock, it was some time before either Ruggedo or Peter had the courage to look up. Then Peter, rubbing the sand and dust from his eyes, raised his head and stared fearfully out to sea. What he saw made him blink with astonishment. The sea had turned itself upside down and on top of the waves, and almost touching Ruggedo's island, lay a long gleaming stretch of sea bottom.

Crystal caverns and sea grottos, coral walls and castles glittered and shimmered in the last rays of the setting sun and, rushing toward the edges of the strange morass was every sort of sea creature Peter ever had imagined. Giant fish wallowed desperately toward the sides and hurled themselves back into the water. Peter rubbed his eyes again to be sure he was not dreaming and, as a golden haired mermaid plunged boldly from the window of a coral castle, he made a grab for Ruggedo. But Ruggedo was already on his crooked little legs.

"Come on! Come on!" wheezed the old Gnome King frantically. "Can't you see it's a way off the island?"

In a daze, Peter ran after him and jumped across the small stretch of water separating their island from the mysterious sea country. It extended as far ahead as they could see.

"Hurry! Hurry!" urged Ruggedo, stumbling over slippery rocks and pausing every few moments to disentangle himself from the oozy arms of some clutching sea plant. "It may go straight to the shores of Ev!" panted the gnome, giving no attention to the frightful sea monsters who were rushing past him in an effort to fling themselves back into the water. "Come on! Come on!"

Shuddering a little, as he collided with an octopus, Peter came. Now they were wading knee deep in green slime, with lobsters, crabs, turtles, jiggers and jelly fish squirming and wiggling uncomfortably against their legs.

Peter wanted to stop at the first coral castle, but Ruggedo ran scornfully past. An old Merman, sitting sadly on the top step, reminded Peter of his grandfather. He wanted to stop and sympathize with the old gentleman, but fearing to be left alone in so scaresome and strange a country, he hurried after the Gnome King. Then Peter saw that which made all else fade from his mind. It was the battered hulk of an old ship, resting against the side of a green sea cavern. It was overgrown with sea moss and barnacles, but the name, in raised letters of pure gold, was still visible.

"Blunderoo!" breathed Peter softly. Then snatching at Ruggedo's coat-tails forced him to stop.

"Let's go aboard!" puffed Peter. "I'll bet we'll find all sorts of useful things. Oh Jimminee! Look! It's a pirate ship!"

Peter pointed to the gold skull and cross bones below the ship's name, his voice trembling with eagerness. Even Ruggedo's eyes began to snap and sparkle with excitement.

"That would mean treasure chests," muttered the old gnome greedily. There was a rusty chain ladder hanging over the ship's side and, seizing the lowest rung, Peter swung himself up and in less than no time had reached the ship's deck. How long it had lain at the bottom of the sea was hard to say, but the planks were water soaked and rotten and everything was crumbling with rust and decay. As the Gnome King dropped down beside Peter, a thunderous explosion shook the boards beneath their feet.

"Another one!" roared Ruggedo, clapping his hands over his ears.

"Another what?" shouted Peter, who was not quite sure what had happened in the first place.

"Sea quake!" quavered the gnome, cowering

back against the ship's cabin. And Ruggedo was right. For a moment longer the strange stretch of sea bed quivered on the surface of the waves. Then, with a splash, grind and rumble, it went crashing back to the bottom and the hungry waves of the Nonestic Ocean tossed and tumbled over the place where it had been.

Now the same terrific shock that hurled the sea land back to the depths of the ocean dislodged the crumbling old pirate wreck and hurled it high into the air. With a shattering smack it smote the churning waters, rocked violently backward and forward, finally righting itself.

"Well, I'll be scuppered!" Letting go of the ring in the cabin door to which he had clung during the whole excitement, Ruggedo slid down to a sitting position on the deck. Peter, with one arm hooked about the ship's railing, was so surprised to find himself alive that he did not speak for several moments.

"Well!" he coughed finally, "at least we have a boat!"

"If we hadn't come aboard we'd have been at the bottom of the sea by this time," shuddered Ruggedo, as Peter sank down beside him. "I believe you've brought me good luck, boy, and when I reach my kingdom I'll make you general of all my armies."

"Thanks," murmured Peter, smiling faintly, "but I'll have to be getting back to Philadelphia. My grandfather will be worried, besides I'm captain of our baseball team and there's a big game on soon."

"Would you rather be captain of a baseball team than an army?" asked Ruggedo, staring at the little boy in real amazement. He didn't know just what a baseball team was, but felt that it could not compare with his army of gnomes.

"Of course," answered Peter, in a matter of fact voice, "but if we're going to get anywhere we'll have to steer the ship." The sun had sunk down into the sea by this time and it was growing darker and darker. Stepping carefully along the rail, for the ship was still plunging and pitching terribly, Peter made a careful survey. But the rudder was gone, the masts crumbled to mere stumps and not a vestige of the sails remained.

"We'll have to drift," called Peter resignedly. Scarcely hearing him, the old gnome nodded. Already a hundred plans were skimming through his wicked little head—plans to reinstate himself as Metal Monarch, revenge himself upon Ozma and Dorothy and destroy once and for all the Emerald City of Oz. The tides of the Nonestic Ocean were very strong, and he felt that sooner or later they would be carried to the shores of Ev, under the surface of which lay his own vast dominions. Directly across the Deadly Desert from Ev, lay Oz, and when he reached his own kingdom some means of crossing the desert would have to be devised.

While Ruggedo was planning all this, Peter was busily exploring the ship. He would have liked to descend into the hold of the pirate vessel, but it was already too dark to venture down, and as he was very hungry, he began to look around for something to eat. Fortunately the decks were still full of wiggling sea creatures that had failed to get back in the water after the sea quake. Peter threw most of them overboard, keeping only three tiny fish for his dinner. These he killed, cleaned and scaled with his pocket knife and, borrowing Ruggedo's pipe which quite miraculously had stayed lit, kindled a small fire in an iron pot and broiled them most satisfactorily.

Ruggedo refused to share Peter's dinner, crunching up instead a handful of pebbles he had in his pocket. As the moon rose the sea

grew calmer and, riding up and down the silvered waves, the strange ship mates sat conversing together. Delighted to be off the lonely island, impressed by Peter's enterprise and spirit, Ruggedo had grown almost friendly. He listened quite pleasantly, while Peter told how the balloon bird had carried him off and then in his turn related a bit of his own history. He first explained to the little boy how Dorothy had captured his magic belt, which seemed to be his most treasured possession, and how she had given it to Ozma. Pulling away at his pipe, he spoke of his many efforts to recover his property, but always, it seemed, through no fault of his own, he had been defeated. After his last attempt he related how Ozma had banished him to the lonely island where Peter had found him.

"Well, why bother with the belt?" asked Peter, a little sleepily, as the gnome paused to

knock the ashes from his pipe. "If you have all the riches you say you have, and are ruler over five hundred thousand gnomes, why do you need this belt?"

"Because it is my most magic possession," explained Ruggedo impatiently. "With the magic belt one can change people into any shape or form whatsoever and transport them where one desires. And don't you see that so long as Ozma has this belt, I am in her power?"

"I suppose so," yawned Peter, but he couldn't help reflecting, from what he had read of Ozma and what he already knew of Ruggedo, that the magic belt was far safer with the little fairy ruler of Oz.

"Why did Dorothy take it from you in the first place?" he inquired drowsily.

"Just because I wanted to transform her and

a few of those useless Oz people into ornaments for my palace," complained Ruggedo in a grieved voice.

"Oh!" murmured Peter and, chuckling a little to himself, curled into a more comfortable position. The deck was hard and wet, but Peter, thinking over the strange events of the day, did not even notice. Up to now, he had believed in the usual things of life, like grandfathers, school, baseball, circuses, vacations in summer, plenty of friends and fun. To suddenly be confronted by balloon birds, gnomes, fairy kingdoms and sea quakes was terribly confusing. Peter tried his best to figure it all out but, lulled by the motion of the ship and the monotonous drone of Ruggedo's voice, he finally fell into a deep slumber.

Ruggedo Discovers Pirate's Treasure

CHAPTER 6

WHEN Peter awakened, the sun was already high in the heavens and the sea a glittering, dancing expanse of blue. Stretching his arms joyously, Peter bounded to his feet, not even minding the little stiffness he felt from his long sleep on deck. The ship was rolling along comfortably with the current, and Ruggedo was nowhere in sight. Tiptoeing over to the cabin, Peter peered in the window, but he was not there.

"He's gone below, I guess," decided Peter, and started down the broken ladder that led into the ship's hold. The port holes, still overgrown with moss and sea weed, let in only a dim, green light but, even so, Peter could see that the walls were hung with rusty swords and muskets, while all about the sides stood old iron sea chests and boxes and rotting sacks, spilling out their gleaming contents of gold and silver coins. Before the largest sea chest, crouched the old Gnome King. He was crooning happily to himself and running his fingers through the sparkling jewels that filled the chest to the very top.

"Well!" exclaimed Peter, pausing with both hands on his hips, "this is a find!"

"I found it first! I found it first!" babbled Ruggedo. "They're mine, Peter, all mine! You may have the gold pieces," he finished jealously. Disgusted with the greedy old gnome, Peter shrugged his shoulders. The gold pieces seemed more desirable anyway. Giving no further attention to Ruggedo, he sank down before one of the bulging sacks and began planning what he should do with his treasure. First, he would build a splendid club house for the team, with hot and cold showers, and next he would buy himself and the gang motorcycles, ponies and canoes! His grandfather should have a new automobile and twenty-five pair of specs, so he'd always have one pair handy. After that—

Clasping his knees and fixing his eyes dreamily upon the beamed ceiling, Peter fell into such pleasant reveries that it was nearly 10 o'clock before he so much as thought of breakfast. Then he suddenly realized he was dreadfully thirsty and went hurrying up the ladder in search of water and provisions. "I hope there are some left," muttered Peter anxiously, "something in tins or bottles that the salt water hasn't got into."

The cabin was a mass of wreckage but opening from that was a small narrow pantry that had evidently been the ship's galley. The shelves had rotted and fallen to the floor. Sand and shells sifted back and forth with the motion of the boat, but in the darkest corner Peter found a heap of casks and tins. Seizing one of the square boxes and a cask, Peter raced out on deck and after some trouble managed to uncork the strangely shaped vessel.

Ah! Water! Sparkling, cold and clear! Peter almost emptied the cask, then, knocking open a box with a piece of wreckage, he found it full of hard, salty ship's biscuits. Smiling to think how long this breakfast had been waiting for him, Peter ate heartily, for when you are hungry even a stale biscuit tastes delicious. Satisfied at last, he took the biscuits and cask below.

Without even a "thank you," Ruggedo gulped down the water and gobbled up the biscuits, which were hard enough to suit even him. Then, wiping his mouth upon his ragged sleeve, he fell to fingering the pirate's jewels again, bending as lovingly over the sea chest as a mother bends over a cradle. After several unsuccessful attempts to draw Ruggedo into a conversation, Peter gave up and went poking around the great dim interior to see what else he could find. Shreds that were once the pirates' coats clung to the nails on the wall and below one of these nails Peter picked up a small metal bound book. Water had blurred all the first pages but, carrying it up to the light, Peter found the last page quite legible. It was the Pirate Chief's diary and, thrilled to his last bone, Peter pored over the pirate's final entry.

"I, Polacky, the Plunderer," said the thin, angular writing, "did this day capture the Island of Ashangabad, taking from the islanders ten chests of gold, three bags of silver, the crown and jewels of state, together with the magic casket of Soob, the Sorcerer. The treasure will I divide, but the magic appliances hold for myself in case of mutiny or capture."

As he read, Peter could almost see the swaggering old Pirate Chief and his men

swarming over the strangely named and defenseless little island. There were some further remarks about the winds and tides, but what interested Peter was the magic casket. "I do wonder what he did with it?" mused the little boy. "Maybe there might be some magic in it that would take me back to Philadelphia." Deciding to say nothing of his discovery to Ruggedo, Peter went below and began a systematic search, poking behind the great chests and bags and tapping on the dank walls for secret cupboards or hollow boards. He had completely circled the treasure room without any success, and was standing on the spot where he picked up the diary, before he made any progress at all. Then, looking down, he noticed that the plank beneath his feet was raised up higher than the others. It might easily have been swollen out of place by the action of the water but, bending down, Peter began to pry at the board. At the second tug it came up altogether, revealing a square, box-like enclosure. In the enclosure lay a small carved casket of jade, a ruby key on top.

Forgetting the necessity for caution, Peter gave a shriek of excitement and, falling upon his knees before the opening, reached eagerly down for the magic box. To fit the key in the lock and open the casket was the work of but a moment. He was a bit disappointed to find what looked like a package of grey gauze, a small uncut emerald and an ivory box with a few directions on the lid. Placing the smaller objects on the floor beside him, Peter unrolled the grey package. It proved to be a long, misty cape, and on the collar was a tiny tag stitched in green.

"The Flying Cloak of Invisibility," announced the tag. "Renders wearer invisible and takes him wheresoever he desires to go."

With a sharp exclamation of delight, Peter arose and was about to fling the magic cloak around him when it was snatched roughly from behind. It was the old Gnome King, of course. For several minutes he had been peering over Peter's shoulder and had also read the legend on the green tag.

"Take me to the Emerald City!" shouted Ruggedo, wrapping himself in the misty folds

of the gray garment. Too startled to even try to recover his property, Peter stood blinking at the old gnome. But he neither disappeared nor whirled off in a cloud of silver dust, as Peter had expected him to do. In fact, nothing happened to him at all.

"What kind of a miserable mumpish magician made this?" stormed Ruggedo, dragging off the cloak and holding it up to the light.

"Well, you had no business to take it in the first place," burst out Peter angrily. "I found the magic casket and the cloak is mine! What good would it have done, any way, if it had carried you to the Emerald City?" he continued more calmly. "You would have left all this treasure behind and had no one to help you capture your belt."

"That's so," admitted Ruggedo, sitting down with the cloak in his lap. "If I had gone you would have taken all the jewels for yourself."

"You bet I would." Folding his arms Peter stared sternly down at the mean little gnome. "Why can't you play fair?" he demanded indignantly.

"Well, weren't you going to fly back to Philadelphia and leave me?" asked Ruggedo triumphantly. "Hah! Hah! You're no better than I am. That's why I like you," he finished maliciously.

Peter blushed a little at the Gnome King's shrewd guess. He had been going to wish himself back to Philadelphia, but pretending not to care, he swept up the other treasures from the magic box and put them into his pocket.

"If you keep the cloak, I shall keep these!" he announced firmly, "and I know why the cloak won't work, too!"

"Why?" In spite of himself, Ruggedo's voice trembled with eagerness.

"Oh—because!" Smiling provokingly and whistling a careless tune, Peter climbed up the ladder. Ruggedo was after him in a flash.

"Tell me!" begged the gnome in his most coaxing voice. "Don't you realize that with the magic cloak I can fly into Ozma's palace and recover my belt without being detected. And when I do," he promised earnestly, "I'll transport you immediately back to Philadelphia—you and all the gold pieces."

"Promise?" Ruggedo nodded so vigorously his hair blew backward and forward seven times.

"All right then," agreed Peter, leaning against the rail of the Blunderoo. "It won't fly because it's torn." Holding the cloak up, Ruggedo saw that Peter was right. There was a large hole in the back and a rent reaching from the collar to the hem.

"Huh, my gnomes can soon mend that," boasted Ruggedo in relief, "and then let Miss Ozma of Oz look to her crown! I'll fly to the Emerald City, steal my belt, and I'll turn her to a canary and clap her into a gold cage. I'll clap them all into cages!" roared Ruggedo, beginning to bounce up and down like a rubber ball. "There won't be one emerald left upon the other, when I get through with them.

Banish me for five years! Take away my Kingdom! I'll show them!"

Forgetting all about Peter, the old Gnome King stamped, shrieked and threatened till the little boy in disgust retired to the other side of the ship. He could easily have taken the cloak away from Ruggedo, but wisely decided to wait. "If we ever do reach this Kingdom of his and the cloak is properly mended I'll take it myself, fly to the Emerald City and warn Ozma that the Gnome King is free," resolved Peter, staring dreamily at the tumbling blue waves. "And once in the Emerald City, Ozma will surely send me back to Philadelphia with the magic belt." Having settled all this to his satisfaction, the little boy pulled out the other possessions of Soob, the Sorcerer. The emerald was covered with strange markings, but Peter could make nothing of them, so he put it back into his pocket and opened the ivory box.

"In case of extreme danger, plant these," advised a pink slip on top of the box. "These" proved to be two onions, or at least they looked like onions. Peter had hoped to find something exciting, like a wishing ring, and putting the onions back, he closed the box with a little sigh. Then, clasping his hands behind his head, he fell to thinking about the pirates and wondering why there were no bones on board.

"They must have taken to the small boats and escaped when the Blunderoo sank," concluded Peter and, having disposed of this question, began wondering what his friends in Philadelphia were doing. He was sorry indeed to have his grandfather worried by his absence, but could not help feeling a little important at the commotion it must be causing. "They've probably called in the police by now," mused Peter, and he hoped that when his grandfather gave his picture to the reporters he would remember to mention that Peter was Captain of the A. P. Baseball Team. In fancy, he saw the large headlines in the morning papers when the news of his final return did get out.

" 'Young Philadelphia Boy Finds Treasure Ship and Saves the Emerald City of Oz!' That wouldn't be bad," thought Peter, and was going over in his mind just how he would describe the sea quake and his other strange adventures when a loud screech from Ruggedo called him to the side of the ship.

"Land!" shouted the Gnome King, with an excited wave toward the west. And it was land. Rolling gently in with the tide, the Blunderoo was approaching a long shallow beach.

"We'll probably go aground," exclaimed Peter, looking anxiously over the side. "It's a good thing the waves are not any larger. What country do you suppose it is, Rug?" Ruggedo had been staring intently ahead and now jumped at least three feet into the air.

"Why, it's Ev!" croaked the Gnome King, hoarse with delight. "Ev! Ev! Ev! The most

beautiful country in the world. My country, Peter!"

"Looks like a wilderness to me," puffed the little boy, but even Peter felt strangely elated and gay. He had not really believed the old gnome's story of his vast dominions, but if this was Ev, he must have been telling the truth. "I don't see any castle!" he murmured, leaning far out over the rail.

"Underground!" panted Ruggedo. "Caverns! Caves! Labyrinths and everything. Wait till you see them, Peter. You'll never want to go back to Philadelphia again. Wait!"

Kaliko Falls as King of Gnomes

CHAPTER 7

EVERY wash and slap of the waves sent the battered old hull of the Blunderoo nearer to shore and, at last, with a tired groan, it stuck its nose into the sand and, listing over sideways, came to a creaky stop.

"Have you the cloak?" asked Peter, one leg already over the rail. Ruggedo held up the small gray package, but looked doubtfully at the foaming waves below.

"How are we going to get to the beach?" he frowned uneasily.

"Lived here all your life and can't swim?" exclaimed Peter. "Great goldfish! Come on, I'll help you," he added impatiently, as the gnome continued to stare uncertainly down at the water. Hurrying down the ladder, Peter dropped easily into the sea, and after a good bit of coaxing, Ruggedo slipped in after him. Taking a firm hold on the gnome's long whiskers and with Ruggedo sputtering and sizzling like a hot coal in a dish pan, Peter struck out for shore. It was soon shallow enough for them to wade and in exactly three minutes from the time the Blunderoo grounded, they stood on the barren shores of Ev.

Forgetting his discomfort, for gnomes like water about as much as cats, the metal monarch began to run as fast as his crooked legs would carry him toward a group of little hills. Looking round without much enthusiasm at the dreary waste of sand and cactus, Peter followed more slowly. His only plan was to keep a sharp watch over Ruggedo and, as soon as the cloak was repaired, to take it away from him and fly to the Emerald City.

"I do hope Ozma can transport the treasure to Philadelphia with me," sighed Peter, quickening his steps as Ruggedo disappeared behind a particularly large rock. He half expected the gnome would try to slip away from him but, to tell the truth, Ruggedo was more kindly disposed toward Peter than toward any mortal he had ever met. He admired Peter's courage and felt that his good fortune was largely due to the boy's enterprise and spirit. Besides, Ruggedo wished to show off his immense dominions and treasure caves, so, as Peter rounded the rock, he took his hand and pressed a hidden spring in the crevice. Instantly a huge door swung inward and they found themselves in a long, dim tunnel.

"I wonder if Kaliko still thinks he is King!" wheezed Ruggedo, pattering along ahead of Peter. Kaliko had been appointed to rule in Ruggedo's place and had been promoted from Royal Chamberlain to King of the Gnomes. "Ha! Ha!" laughed Ruggedo maliciously. "He'll be as pleased as a Gundersnutch when he sees me back!"

Peter answered nothing to this, for he was too interested in the underground world in which he found himself to pay much attention to the old gnome's remarks. As they proceeded, a perfect network of passageways opened from the main tunnel, the sides, walls and ceilings gleaming with sparkling jewels. Thousands of gnomes with pick axes were busily at work digging out the gems and they did not even look up as Peter and Ruggedo passed them. Blazing rubies and emeralds set in tall stands lighted up the strange caverns and Peter's heart began to pound with excitement as the passageway broadened out into a richly carpeted hallway. Presently they found themselves before a grilled golden door with a diamond knob. Without pausing, Ruggedo turned the knob, opened the door and simply rushed into his former throne room. On a huge round ruby, hollowed out to form a seat, a thin, nervous gnome sat reading a silver sheet about as thick as our morning papers. It was the Gnome Man's Daily, and as Peter and Ruggedo burst noisily into the royal chamber, he dropped the silver sheet and looked up with an exclamation of alarm.

"You!" gasped Kaliko, as if he could not believe his own senses.

"Who else?" snickered Ruggedo, winking at Peter. "I'll thank you for my crown, you robber. Take it right off your Kalikoko. Quick now! Hand it over!"

"Ozma will never consent to this," stammered Kaliko, holding to the crown with both hands.

"Ozma has nothing to do with me now," announced Ruggedo calmly. "I have magic stronger than Ozma's and if you don't hop off that throne, I'll turn you to a ball and bounce you off!"

Peter listened in amazement to Ruggedo's boasts, but Kaliko seemed to believe every word. With quaking knees, he descended the steps of the throne and held out the crown to his former master.

"Ha! Ha!" roared Ruggedo, snatching the crown and clapping it jauntily on the back of his head. "You're enough to make an alligator laugh, Kaliko. So brave! So kingly! But don't stand there gibbering like a dunce. If you are no longer King, you are still Royal Chamberlain, and this is Peter, future general of my armies!" Tripping merrily up the steps of the throne, Ruggedo waved toward the little boy. "We will shortly make a journey to the Emerald City,"

he announced grandly, "but right now we desire refreshment. Lunch for two," he commanded, putting his finger tips together and leaning back comfortably. "And, by the way," he added as an afterthought, "there is a pirate ship on the beach. Have it unloaded and the treasure stored in the silver grotto. Then order me a dozen new suits and send in the Royal Wizard."

At each command, Kaliko bowed meekly, and as Ruggedo picked up the ruby scepter lying on the arm of the throne, he ducked and ran out the door, for Ruggedo, as a mere matter of habit, had flung the scepter after him.

"A blockhead!" sniffed Ruggedo contemptuously, "but didn't I manage him well?"

"He's not very brave," admitted Peter, sitting on the edge of the crystal rocking chair, "but how are you going to get along without any magic? Suppose the gnomes don't want you back again?"

"One thing at a time! One thing at a time!" beamed Ruggedo, in such a fine humor at his unexpected turn of luck, he felt almost pleasant. "Let's not worry till we have to, General." Peter couldn't help smiling at his new title and, surveying himself in the long mirror, wondered how he would look in a gnome uniform. But at this juncture they were interrupted by the entrance of the Royal Wizard. He looked frightened and anxious, and Peter could see from his manner that the old Gnome King was no great favorite with his former subjects.

"Well, Potaroo!" grinned Ruggedo, taking up the pipe Kaliko had been smoking, "what have you been inventing in my absence?"

"Flying dishes," croaked the magician, looking curiously at Peter. "They do away with extra servants, fly backward and forward with the food and wash and dry themselves as well."

"Very good!" puffed Ruggedo, complacently. "Well, here's another little job for you." Drawing out the cloak, he handed it down to the wizened old gnome. "Just mend this,"

ordered Ruggedo carelessly, "and have it back by three o'clock." Spreading the cloak across his knees, Potaroo examined it carefully all over. Then backing away from the throne he shook his head.

"That, your Majesty, is impossible," he

muttered uneasily. "This cloak cannot be mended by gnome magic."

"No magic at all?" gasped Peter, disappointed beyond words, while Ruggedo glared angrily.

"I command you to mend it!" screamed the hot-tempered little King, looking angrily around for something to throw at the wizard.

"That makes no difference," quavered Potaroo, backing still farther. "This cloak cannot be mended properly anywhere but in the Kingdom of Patch."

"And where is Patch?" demanded Ruggedo, emitting a perfect cloud of pipe smoke.

"In the Winkie Country of Oz, just below the Kingdom of Ann of Oogaboo," exclaimed Potaroo, looking longingly over his shoulder at the door.

"Very well," snapped Ruggedo disagreeably, "you may go, but next time your magic fails to work you'll be turned to a door mat. A door mat, do you understand? Hah! Hah! A door mat to stand under my feet. See!" Ruggedo laughed wickedly, and the poor wizard, mumbling his sorrow, rushed from the throne room.

"Rubyation!" blustered Ruggedo, as the door closed on Potaroo. "Now we'll have to go to Patch."

"Well, isn't that on the way to the Emerald City?" inquired Peter, very much amused by all that had happened.

"Yes," acknowledged Ruggedo, "I suppose it is, but here comes lunch! Ah! I'm hungry enough to eat a billy goat stuffed with soldier buttons!"

Preceded by two gnomes carrying a huge golden tray, Kaliko came stepping timidly into the room. Ruggedo had the usual gnome fare of ground rocks, pebble pie and muddy coffee; but for Peter, Kaliko had brought a small steak, fried potatoes and ice cream. After the hard sea biscuit, this tasted perfectly delicious, and Peter, not knowing what strange adventures lay ahead, ate every scrap. Ruggedo, too, enjoyed his luncheon and amused himself by throwing the dishes at Kaliko as he finished with them. Peter wondered why the flying dishes were not in use, but feeling sorry for the old wizard decided not to ask.

"You may now pack us up a lunch," announced Ruggedo, as he swallowed the last of his coffee. "We're starting for the Emerald City almost at once."

"How are you going to cross the desert?" inquired Kaliko. Angry as he was at the old Gnome King, he could not help feeling curious about his plans.

"Magic! Old Cauliflower! Magic! How do you suppose I got off the island?" wheezed Ruggedo haughtily. "Don't stand there stuttering. Fetch me a new suit and hurry along with the lunch."

Shrugging his thin shoulders, and turning up his eyes, Kaliko did as he was told, and in less than an hour Peter and the Gnome King were wending their way over the rocky hills of

Ev. Ruggedo had the magic cloak tucked carefully under his arm and Peter carried a small basket of provisions.

"How *are* we going to cross this desert?" asked Peter, looking with interest down toward the beach where the gnomes were busily at work unloading the treasure from the Blunderoo.

"I don't know," confessed Ruggedo quite frankly, "but if Kaliko had discovered I had not magic enough to cross the desert, he would have roused the gnomes and kicked us out of the kingdom."

"Is there no other way to Oz?" sighed Peter. He was growing a little anxious about ever reaching Philadelphia in time for the baseball game.

"Nope!" puffed the Gnome King, trudging along sturdily. "The Deadly Desert surrounds the whole country. It's supposed to keep people out of Oz," he finished with a malicious wink. "But it has been crossed before and can be crossed again, though I'm sure I don't know how."

The entrance of the Gnome King's caverns was quite near the edge of the Deadly Desert, so it was not long before they reached this dangerous expanse of burning sand and sat down on a boulder to try and devise some means of crossing over.

"Can't you think of anything?" snapped Ruggedo, as Peter sat kicking his heels against the boulder. "If this silly old cloak weren't torn, I'd skim across in no time. A skudge on those pesky pirates anyway! Sa—ay?" Opening his eyes very wide, Ruggedo thrust his face close to Peter's. "What else was in that casket?"

"Only a couple of onions and an emerald," answered Peter listlessly.

"Let's see 'em!" Bounding off the boulder, the Gnome King held out his hand. Peter produced the strangely marked stone first.

"Command it to carry us across the desert," advised the Gnome King, after trying unsuccessfully to decipher the markings on the sorcerer's stone. So Peter closed his eyes and commanded the emerald to carry them across the desert. They waited for several minutes, then, when nothing happened, Peter opened the ivory box and showed Ruggedo the two magic bulbs.

"In case of extreme danger, plant these." Ruggedo read these directions with a puzzled frown, then snapping his fingers began to skip with excitement. "Why don't you plant 'em?" he squealed impatiently. "Plant 'em, General! Plant 'em!"

"But we're not in extreme danger," objected Peter reasonably enough.

"We're not!" yelled Ruggedo, tugging at his beard. "Why, boy, you don't know what extreme danger is. We have to cross that desert, don't we? Well, just put one foot on that sand and you'll go up like a puff of smoke. Don't you call that extreme danger?" Peter argued a while longer, then, as Ruggedo insisted and there really seemed nothing else to do, he scooped

out two holes in the ground at his feet, dropped in the magic roots and covered them with mud and sand. Stepping back a few paces, they waited eagerly for what would happen. First came a sharp explosion. Then two great green plants burst through the surface of the earth. They were about three times the size of Peter and, as he watched, the outer leaves opened downward, disclosing round plush seats within. Peter looked questioningly over at Ruggedo, but the gnome, being more experienced than Peter in magic, had jumped into one plant and seated himself on the plush cushion. A little doubtfully, Peter jumped into the other.

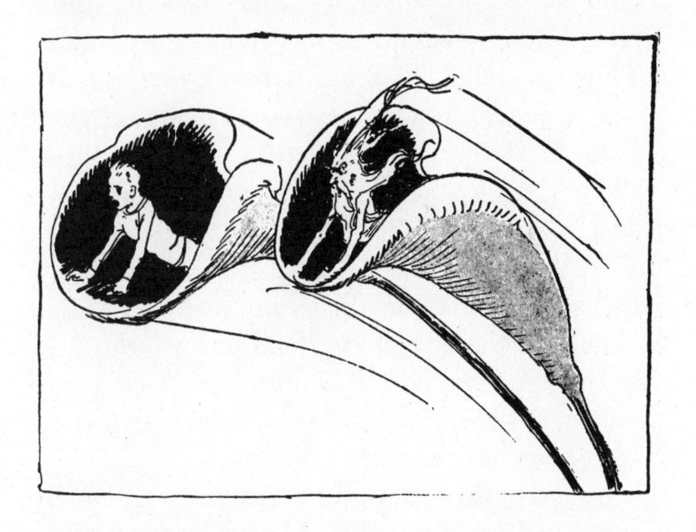

"Just like an elevator," thought Peter, as the bulb grew rapidly upward, shooting higher and higher on its long, pliant stem. "But I don't see what good growing up will do," he muttered, peering giddily out between the green leaves. Whether he saw or not, the stem of the bulb continued to grow. Clouds flew by with dazzling swiftness. Peter was all prepared to bump his head on the ceiling of the sky when the long stem began to arch downward. Suppose it broke and dropped him on the burning sands of the deadly desert! With a violent shudder, Peter closed his eyes, and as he did, the stem with a final spurt turned the strange elevator in which Peter was riding completely upside down, and out fell the little boy, heels over eyebrows.

Ruggedo had been served in the same manner but, none the worse for their tumble, they picked themselves up and began looking around. They had fallen in a sunny peach orchard. In the distance they could see the shimmering sand of the dangerous desert, while not far away stood a small, yellow, dome-shaped cottage.

"We'll go there," declared Ruggedo, tucking the magic cloak more carefully under his arm. "We'll go there, General, and inquire the way to the Kingdom of Patch. But remember to say nothing of the plans to capture my belt. We're in the enemy's country now!"

Still dazed from the surprising way in which they had crossed the desert, Peter looked around him with delight. It did not look like the enemy's country to Peter and, picking up a large, luscious peach, he decided then and there that he was going to like the Marvelous Land of Oz.

Peter thought that even the Wizard of Oz, himself, would be interested in the wonderful elevator plants, and decided to tell him all about them when he got to the Emerald City.

CHAPTER 8

AS they walked up the neat pebble path to the little yellow house, Peter tried to remember all he had read about Oz and its curious inhabitants. But nothing he had read prepared him for the next happening. In answer to their knock, the door simply burst open and out came a hand and foot without any body at all. The hand seized Peter's hand, shook it warmly and drew him into the house. The foot gave Ruggedo such a kick, he went flying into a gooseberry bush. Drawn by the hand into a cozy sitting room, Peter stood trembling with uneasiness. In a comfortable chair, smoking a pipe, sat the owner of the cottage, also the owner of the hand and foot, and Peter gave a gasp as they immediately snapped back to their proper places.

"Don't be alarmed," said the stranger in a soft voice and, taking the pipe out of his mouth,

he smiled kindly at the little boy. Peter was not alarmed—he was perfectly petrified and, as the old gentleman's head flew off his body and looked out the window, he dropped into a chair and began to fan himself with his cap. "I thought he'd go away," sighed the head regretfully, "but he's coming into the house. Why do you travel with a bad little creature like that?"

"Because I'm lost," explained Peter, in a slightly shaky voice, turning around to address himself to the head.

"Well, you may find yourself in a heap of trouble, travelling with a gnome. Never trust a gnome," advised the head, coming back to settle on the old gentleman's shoulders. "Ah! Here he comes!"

"Who kicked me?" demanded Ruggedo, glaring all around in a perfect fury. The owner of the cottage made no reply, but as he needed more tobacco for his pipe just then, flung out his hand toward the mantel. The hand sailed through the air like a bird and, seizing the tobacco pouch, set it on the table and then quietly attached itself to the man's wrist. At this odd occurrence, Ruggedo's eyes rolled wildly. Cringing against the wall, he began to move stealthily toward the door.

"Don't go," begged the owner of the cottage blandly. "I'm not especially fond of gnomes, but as you are with this honest lad you may stay. Sit down on that bench there and if I catch you stealing anything, I'll throw my head at you." Pale with terror, Ruggedo did as he was told, while the man's hand, flying off again, closed and locked the door.

"There!" he sighed, leaning back contentedly, "now we can talk without being disturbed and let us start at once with names. My name," he confided proudly, "is Kuma Party, and I have had the curious gift which seems so to astonish you since early childhood. My father was a wizard, practicing magic in the Zamagoochie Country, before the practice of magic was forbidden in Oz, and it is to my father that I attribute my strange come-apartishness." He paused and waited politely for Peter to make some remark, but Peter by this time was simply speechless, so Kuma, with an indulgent smile, went quietly on with his story.

"Being constructed as I am is extremely

convenient," he explained earnestly. "I am never tired or rushed about as ordinary Oz folk are. If I wish to pick the peaches in my orchard, I send my hands to attend to the matter and while they are busily at work I rest myself comfortably at home. If my body is tired and I desire to be amused, I send my head to the nearest village for news and I can often help my less fortunate neighbors by lending them a hand or foot when they are in trouble. Perhaps I can help you?" he suggested, leaning amiably toward Peter. "May I lend you a hand?" he finished graciously.

Now Kuma, in spite of his come-apartishness, seemed so pleasant and jolly that Peter wanted to tell him the whole history of his adventures, but Ruggedo frowned and shook his head, so for the present Peter decided to fall in with the gnome's plans and merely told Kuma his name and asked him the way to Patch.

"Patch?" mused the Winkie thoughtfully. "Why, that's not far from here. It is just below the Kingdom of Queen Ann of Oogaboo, but why not wait till morning? It's growing dark now and besides it's raining." Looking out in surprise, Peter saw that it was raining. He had been so interested in Kuma's story that he had not even heard the patter of raindrops on the roof.

"Better stay," urged Kuma hospitably. "While my hands are preparing the supper, you can tell me some more about your own self and why you are going to Patch."

All during Kuma's conversation, Ruggedo had been wiggling with impatience and now, bouncing to his feet, he motioned for Peter to come along.

"I guess we will have to go," sighed Peter. "Which direction do we take from here, Mr. Party?" The old Winkie looked disapprovingly at the little gnome, then shaking his head and evidently concluding that it was no affair of his, threw out his right arm. It immediately whizzed up stairs, but was back in a moment, a large umbrella hanging in the crook of the elbow and a lantern grasped in the hand.

"Since you must go," said Kuma, rising slowly to his feet, "at least let me point out the way for you and loan you an umbrella."

"It's very kind of you," faltered Peter, ducking in spite of himself as the arm passed over his head on its way to open the door. "Are you sure you can spare it?"

"Oh, yes!" Kuma nodded cheerfully. "I still have one left, you know, and as I'm only going to play checkers this evening, one will be plenty. Goodbye." He smiled, patting Peter kindly on the shoulder. "Remember what I told you about gnomes." He stared sternly down at Ruggedo, and Ruggedo, not daring to meet his eye, scuttled nervously into the garden.

"Maybe I'll see you again," said Peter, and

shaking Kuma's remaining hand stepped reluctantly after the Gnome King.

"I hope so," called Kuma and, with a farewell wave and nod he went in and shut the door. Peter had to run to catch up with Ruggedo. He was already out of the gate and halfway down the road. As he reached the gnome's side, Kuma's arm, holding the umbrella carefully, took its position over their heads.

"Why didn't you stay?" grumbled Peter crossly. "There were lots of things I wanted to ask that man." Really he felt quite provoked with the old gnome.

"Sh-h!" warned Ruggedo, pointing warningly up at the arm over their heads. "Shh-hh!"

"Well, you don't suppose he can hear through his fingers, do you?" teased Peter, and then, because everything did seem so comical and ridiculous, he burst into a loud laugh. "I wish grandfather could see this," gasped the Captain of the A. P. Baseball Team, reaching in his pocket for his handkerchief. "Jimminy, wouldn't it be fine to have an extra arm in a scrap with the fellows!"

Ruggedo was too busy with his own thoughts to pay any attention to Peter's, so for quite a while they walked along in silence. It was pouring steadily, but Kuma's umbrella was so large and his hand held it so carefully, not a drop fell upon the travelers. It was too gloomy to see much of the country but, from the tidy farms and orchards they did glimpse through the curtain of rain, Peter concluded that the Winkie Country must be a very prosperous and delightful place to live in. They had to walk briskly to keep pace with the umbrella, but after an hour or so the rain stopped. The arm stopped also, and after standing about uncertainly and wondering what to do, Peter reached up and closed the umbrella. Then taking a match, which he noticed in the rim of the lantern that swung from Kuma's wrist, he lifted the chimney and lit the wick within. This was evidently what the arm had been waiting for and now it moved confidently a few paces ahead, the forefinger of its hand pointing stiffly in the direction they were to follow. It was quite late by now and the lantern shed a cheery light over the fast darkening road.

Nibbling at the supper Kaliko had packed up for them, Peter and Ruggedo hastened after Kuma's guiding hand.

"I wonder if it will fly back when we come to Patch," mused Peter as they turned off the main road and into a small wood.

"Let's hold on to it," whispered the Gnome King craftily. "We can tie it up somehow and then when I get my magic belt, I'll make it work for me."

"That's a nice way to repay a man for helping us," said Peter angrily. "You ought to be ashamed of yourself."

"Well, I'm not," grunted the Gnome King, pausing to light his pipe, "and if you are going to be general of my armies, you'd better get over these nice ideas and notions. Didn't I hear you say a while ago that you'd like to have an extra arm yourself?"

"I said I'd like to have one, but I never said I'd steal one," answered Peter indignantly.

"Take anything you need," advised Ruggedo, puffing away at his pipe. "That's my motto." Realizing it was useless to argue with so bad a little gnome, Peter kept his own counsel and, fixing his eyes on the bobbing lantern ahead, wondered when they would reach Patch and what it would be like when they did reach it. He hoped there would be no wild animals or bandits upon the road and peered anxiously from side to side as they made their way through the tangled woodland. But without any worse mishap than a tumble over a fallen tree trunk, they came to the end of the wood and struck out across a broad field.

"Tomatoes!" muttered Peter, treading carefully between the plants. Leaning down he picked an especially tempting one and sank his teeth deep into the side. "Ugh!" choked Peter, shuddering with distaste. "It's cotton! What kind of a silly country is this anyway?"

"A cotton country, I s'pose," grinned Ruggedo, greatly amused at Peter's wry face. "Cotton? Why, maybe it's Patch itself!" By the light of Kuma's lantern, they could now see some cottages ahead and the dim outline of a castle.

"Rocks and Rookies!" exulted the Gnome King, waving the cloak over his head. "It won't be long now before I'm ruler of the realm, boy!"

"I thought you just wanted your magic belt," puffed Peter, running anxiously after Ruggedo.

"Oh, grow up!" called the gnome scornfully over his shoulder. "Grow up and don't be so soft. You're a regular Wooshmacushion!" Shooting ahead like an arrow, Kuma's arm now flew so swiftly that it was all they could do to keep up with it. By the time they had reached the castle they had barely enough breath to mount the steps. As they did, the arm, in a business-like manner, set down the lantern and, taking the umbrella in its hand, thumped hard upon the castle door.

"Good!" panted Ruggedo, sinking down on the top step. "That ought to rouse them." When no response came, he jumped up himself and began to kick and pound on the panels. Peter, naturally more polite, had at once put his finger on the bell and they were thus engaged when Piecer and Scrapper, returning from town, turned in at the gate.

"Customers," murmured Scrapper, rubbing his hands in anticipation.

"Wizards!" faltered Piecer, pointing with a trembling finger to the detached arm of Kuma, still beating on the door with the umbrella.

"So much the better! So much the better! Wizards always pay well." Running up the palace steps, the Chief Scrapper of Patch tapped Ruggedo respectfully on the shoulder. "What can we do for you?" asked Scrapper, pulling the castle key from his pocket.

Ruggedo had been expecting attention from the other side of the door and was so startled that he made no answer, but the hand of Kuma immediately dropped the umbrella and shook hands with the Quilty statesman. It then moved quickly on toward Piecer, but Piecer, with a muffled scream, dodged behind a pillar. Snapping its fingers to show that it did not care one way or the other, the hand approached Peter and, after patting him approvingly on the shoulder, slipped a small note into his pocket. Then it shook its finger sternly under Ruggedo's nose, picked up the lantern and umbrella and vanished from view.

Even Scrapper was somewhat dashed at this and, in a slightly choky voice, repeated his question to Ruggedo. Ruggedo was terribly provoked to have the arm escape but, recovering himself quickly, bowed civilly to the two Quilties.

"I have a cloak to be mended," he announced grandly, "and will pay you handsomely for the trouble."

"Certainly! Certainly!" Unlocking the door, Scrapper waved them into the shabby hallway then, lighting a candle, bade them follow him.

"I'll take you to the Queen," said Scrapper importantly, "and while she is entertaining you I will fetch our most skillful needlewoman."

As for Peter, he was so excited over the adventure with Kuma's hand, he could think of nothing else.

Queen Scraps Meets Peter

CHAPTER 9

IT IS hard to say who was more astonished, when Scrapper opened the door of the sitting room and ushered in Peter and Ruggedo. The Patchwork Girl, who had been expecting a rescue party headed by the Scarecrow or some of her other old friends, stared in disbelief and horror at the King of the Gnomes. Ruggedo was so surprised to see Scraps outside of the Emerald City, and so disconcerted to know that she was the Queen on whom he must depend for favor, that he nearly ran out of the room. Scraps knew all about the wicked little gnome, and had even been present when he was banished to Runaway Island. Peter thought of all the curious people he had met so far, and this Queen was the most curious and comical. But as they all kept their thoughts to themselves, Scrapper noticed nothing amiss.

"Kindly entertain this customer until I return," ordered Scrapper and, with a curt nod at the Queen, went out and locked the door behind him. For a second longer Scraps and the Gnome King stared fixedly at one another. Then the Patchwork Girl, snatching off her steel-rimmed spectacles, groaned:

"Ruggedo, as I live, oh my land!
How'd he get off of that island?"

"That's my affair," answered the Gnome King in a surly voice. "How do you happen to be Queen of Patch, I should like to know?"

"That's my affair," sniffed Scraps haughtily. "But I know you are up to some mischief. Boy," she demanded, turning severely to Peter, "where did you meet this robber and what is he planning to do?"

Peter shuffled his feet uncomfortably, hardly knowing what to say. He was anxious for the magic cloak to be mended, for how else was he to reach the Emerald City and warn Ozma of her danger. If he told the whole truth they might both be thrown into prison, or so thought Peter then. Ruggedo was waiting nervously for his reply, and as the little boy mumbled out a few words about being lost and trying to find his way back home, the Gnome King sighed with relief.

"Why get so excited?" wheezed Ruggedo in a conciliatory voice. "I merely want to have my cloak mended and was told it could be done here better than anywhere else. What's wrong about that?"

"It's wrong for you to be off the island," insisted Scraps. "You know perfectly well you were banished forever. Oh, for an egg! For a dozen eggs!" At the mention of eggs, Ruggedo turned quite pale under his wrinkled gray skin and, as Peter looked at the two in perplexity, Scrapper returned bringing an old Quilty grandame with him. She was angry to be summoned at so late an hour and, grumbling crossly, snatched the cloak from Ruggedo's hand. Seating herself in a low chair by the candle, she opened her sewing box and began to stitch so rapidly that her needle fairly flashed through the air.

"Now then," murmured Scrapper, smiling in satisfaction, "as to the price?"

"I command you to arrest this creature," interrupted the Patchwork Girl, rushing up to the Chief Scrapper. "Don't you realize that he is the former King of the Gnomes and that he has tried to capture Oz at least a dozen times?"

"A king?" exclaimed Scrapper, clasping his hands rapturously. "Why, how we are honored! Have a chair, your Majesty! Have a cushion! Have—"

"Oh, have some sense!" screamed Scraps, while Ruggedo sidled closer to the old woman who was mending his cloak. "If you let him go he'll try to capture the Emerald City. He always does.

> "He's mean, he's cruel, he's dangerous,
> He'll ruin Oz and all of us!"

"Nonsense!" sniffed Scrapper, giving the Patchwork Girl a push. "He is our honored customer, and you may be the Queen here, but remember, I'm the boss. Keep quiet or I'll send for the Scissor Bird."

"Wouldn't this make your ear ache?" Peter jumped at the new voice and, peering around in the direction it had come from, saw a little bear peeking out of a chest. It was Grumpy, of course, and, as Peter continued to stare at him, he retired into the chest and closed the lid. But the Gnome King, encouraged by Scrapper's treatment of the Patchwork Girl, puffed out his cheeks quite cheerfully.

"You are a man of judgment," he observed in a flattering tone. "Be assured that I will remember this kindness, but what can I do to repay you for mending the cloak?" Scrapper looked thoughtful for a moment while the Patchwork Girl continued to mutter and scold under her breath.

"Is this your slave?" he inquired at last, turning inquisitively to Peter. Ruggedo seemed a little surprised, but to Peter's disgust and astonishment immediately nodded briskly.

"Well, then," said Scrapper, "suppose you give us the boy in payment for mending the cloak. Our Queen is not quick enough to do all the work here and he looks strong and willing."

"I'm not his slave!" burst out Peter wrathfully. "I'll not stay here, you old simpleton." But the more he shouted the more Ruggedo nodded and smiled at Scrapper.

"Never mind," whispered the Patchwork Girl, as Peter, on his way to the door, bumped into her, "never mind, I'll help you." And with this assurance he was forced to be satisfied. Realizing that Ruggedo meant to keep none of his promises, Peter tried to plan a way to get hold of the cloak first. But the Gnome King, pressing close to the old Quilty seamstress, waved him jealously away, and Scrapper, jerking him roughly by the arm, whirled him off into a corner.

And now the cloak was mended. Shaking the threads from its folds the old grandame held it out to Ruggedo. As she did so, Peter rushed forward impetuously, but the gnome was too quick for him. Flinging on the magic garment, Ruggedo vanished from view, only the blue patch on the back of the cloak showing he was still in the room. Scrapper and the others screamed out in alarm, but Peter, throwing up his arm, cried out loudly, "Take him to Zamagoochie!" In a flash the Gnome King was

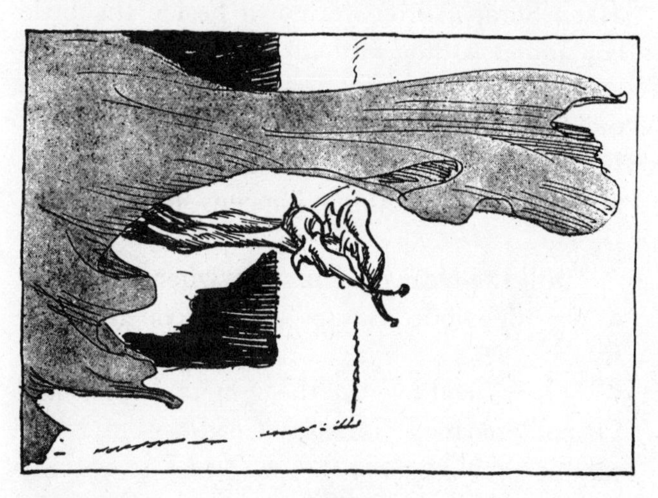

gone, at least the blue patch was gone, and Peter, stamping his foot angrily, turned to the foolish old Quilty. "Now you've done it!" panted the little boy.

"I told you not to help him," cried Scraps, coming over to stand beside Peter. "You'll be sorry for this."

"Oh, keep quiet!" mumbled Scrapper, mopping his forehead with his patched hanky. To tell the truth, the sudden disappearance of the Gnome King had upset him terribly. "I don't see what you're fussing about," he finished fretfully. "Here you have a nice new slave to work for you. Out of my way there!"

Taking the old Quilty woman by the arm, he brushed rudely past Peter, unlocked the door and went out. As the key clicked in the lock, Peter sank down on the floor, the picture of discouragement.

"Why did you say that about Zamagoochie?" asked Scraps, dropping down beside the little boy and regarding him curiously.

"Because it was the first place that came into my head," explained Peter. "Jimminy, but I hope it's a long way from the Emerald City, and I hope something happens to keep him there."

"Will the cloak take him anywhere he wants to go?" demanded Scraps. Peter nodded gloomily.

"Then good-bye to the Emerald City and Ozma!" moaned Scraps. "Good-bye to all of us."

"Yes, but what's to be done with the slave?" Grumpy had lifted the lid of the chest again and was regarding Peter with great interest.

"He's not a slave!" exclaimed Scraps scornfully. "I can tell by his looks, he's a mortal child like Dorothy and Betsy. How did you find your way to Oz, boy?" Peter was anxious to escape from the castle, but when Scraps assured him that there was no present hope of such a thing, he told her all that had happened since the balloon bird carried him off from Philadelphia. As the story progressed, Grumpy climbed out of the chest and sat as close to Peter as he could possibly squeeze.

"Tell him about us!" urged the little bear, as Peter wound up his story with a description of Kuma Party and his guiding hand. Scraps shook her head impatiently, but when Peter added his voice to Grumpy's she introduced the pet of the former Queen and gave a brief description of herself and her happy life at the capital. When Peter heard how she had been kidnapped and forced to do all the castle work, he shook his head sympathetically.

"We'll both run away," declared Peter, resolutely, "and as you know more about Oz than I do, perhaps we'll reach the Emerald City ahead of Ruggedo."

"But first you must escape from the castle," the little bear reminded them sagely. "How will you do that?"

"I wish there had been a little more magic in that casket," sighed Scraps. "All you have

left is the emerald. Let me see the emerald, Peter." Peter pulled out the sorcerer's stone and handed it over to Scraps and, as he did, felt the note that Kuma's hand had thrust into his pocket. Opening it eagerly, Peter followed the Patchwork Girl to the light. But as they reached the center table, the candle which had been burning lower and lower gave a final sputter and went out, leaving them in total darkness.

"Botheration!" cried Peter in exasperation. "Now what shall we do?"

"Go to sleep," yawned the little bear. "Whenever you don't know what to do, go to sleep. That's my advice. Here, lean on me."

"Why don't you?" suggested Scraps, feeling her way carefully back to the rocker. "Mortal folk need rest, but as I do not, I'll sit and plan our escape."

Grumpy's advice did seem sensible and, as

Peter was very tired, he curled down beside the little bear and soon did go to sleep, his head resting comfortably on Grumpy's soft shoulder. In his hand he grasped Kuma's note, and in his dreams imagined himself already in the Emerald City, fighting to defend the little Queen of all Oz.

Escape from Patch at Last

CHAPTER 10

WHEN Peter awakened next morning, he thought for a few moments he was still aboard ship. But he soon realized that the up and down motion he was experiencing was merely the deep breathing of the little bear. Without disturbing Grumpy, he straightened up and rubbed his eyes. Scraps was over by the window turning Soob's emerald over and over in her cotton fingers. Reminded of the letter he had been about to read when the candle went out, Peter felt around till he found Kuma's note. Hurrying over to the Patchwork Girl, he spread it open and quickly read its contents.

"If you ever need a helping hand, send for mine," said the note. "Write directions on this paper and toss into the air."

"Well, hurrah!" exclaimed Peter, showing the note to Scraps. "Kuma will lend us a hand any time we need it."

"Three cheers! Four laughs!
Five grins—a bow!
Send for it quick, I need it now,"

cried the Patchwork Girl. "In a minute I'll have to cook, sweep, dust, scrub and make beds. Why, an extra hand will be wonderful. Send for it, Peter. Send for it right way. You're a slave too, remember."

"I was thinking it might unlock the doors and help us escape," mused the little boy, wrinkling up his brows. "Could you read the markings on the emerald?"

"No," admitted Scraps, handing back the stone, "but keep it safely, Peter. You never know when or where magic will work in this country and we need all the magic we can find to get to the Emerald City before Ruggedo."

"I wonder where he is now?" worried Peter. "Zamagoochie was the country Kuma's father came from, but I wonder where it is and whether Rug is still there or whether he has reached the Emerald City and turned Ozma to a canary?"

"Stop! Stop!" begged Scraps. "Let's stop worrying and try to think. If we send for Kuma's hand now, when all the Quilties are working in the fields, we will soon be captured, even if we escape from the castle. We'll have to wait till night," sighed the Patchwork Girl, "though how I'm going to stand another day here I don't see!"

"Never mind," said Peter sympathetically, "I'll help."

"I'll help, too!" volunteered Grumpy, rolling over on his side and yawning tremendously. "It won't be as bad as growling all the time and that's how I helped Cross Patch!"

"Sh-hh!" warned Scraps, "Here they come! Look out for the Scissor Bird, Peter, he's dreadfully careless with his bill." Thrusting Kuma's note into his pocket and assuming as defiant an attitude as he well could, Peter waited for the door to open, which it presently did. In came Scrapper, the Scissor Bird on his shoulder and Piecer staggering under a great pile of coats and other garments that had been sent in to be mended.

"Good morning, Slave!" Scrapper bowed stiffly to Peter and then to Scraps. "Kindly prepare breakfast, at once!"

"Oh scrapple!" scolded the Patchwork Girl.

"Not scrapple, eggs," said Piecer, setting down his pile of garments. "And when you have finished with breakfast, please sort these."

"Why don't you sort them yourself," suggested Peter boldly, but as the Scissor Bird made a dash in his direction he hastily sprang behind Scraps.

"It's an outrage to expect a Queen to do all the work," began Scraps, settling her spectacles severely. "Ozma never does a stroke of work. Ozma—"

"Ozma?" shrilled the Scissor Bird. "Well,

every time you think you're Ozma, look in the glass. Come along, you lazy creature!" Circling over the Patchwork Girl's head and making playful snips at her yarn, the Scissor Bird drove her ahead of him toward the castle kitchen. Peter and Grumpy followed cautiously, conversing in indignant whispers.

Peter had often been camping and, seeing how terribly unhandy Scraps was with the cooking utensils, he prepared the breakfast himself. Then he set the table and carried the eggs, nicely fried, to the two Quilties, who sat at ease in the shabby dining room. The Scissor Bird ate a saucer of calico scraps and Grumpy a loaf of bread and an apple. After being assured that the Patchwork Girl herself would eat nothing, Peter fried himself an egg and sat down at the kitchen table to enjoy himself. The Scissor Bird was too busy eating to bother them for a moment and, availing himself of this opportunity, Peter began to talk in a low voice to Scraps.

"Why did you wish for a dozen eggs when you first saw Ruggedo?" he asked curiously.

"Because eggs are poison to gnomes," whispered Scraps. "They are more afraid of eggs than of bombshells and they cannot even stay in the same room with one."

"Hm-m!" mused Peter thoughtfully, "I'll remember that. How is it," he asked presently, "that Grumpy can talk?"

"All the animals in Oz talk," explained Scraps in a matter of fact voice. "Just wait till you hear the Cowardly Lion and the Hungry Tiger!"

"Do they live in the Emerald City?" Peter's eyes grew round with interest. Scraps nodded enthusiastically, then noticing that the Scissor Bird had finished, she sprang up and began to clear away the dishes. But Grumpy kindly offered to wash them, so hurrying back into the sitting room, Scraps and Peter fell to sorting old clothes. In one pile they put coats, in another dresses, in a third, trousers, and in a fourth, all the shirts needing new cuffs or collars. Conversation was impossible, for the Scissor Bird was never quiet for a moment and soon Peter's head began to ache from its continuous screeching. Once when he dropped an old cloak, it snipped a lock of his hair and when he struck out at it angrily, it nearly nipped a piece off his ear.

To Scrapper and Piecer, sitting in the doorway, this proved highly amusing and, glaring at the old Quilties, Peter resolved to send for Kuma's hand at the first opportunity. Grumpy had finished the dishes and, with a gingham apron tied round his waist, was energetically sweeping the floor.

"Don't you care," he whispered comfortingly as he passed Peter. "Today won't last forever!" It seemed like forever to Peter and Scraps, but

as they came to the bottom of the pile the Patchwork Girl made a startling discovery. Between a faded vest and a quilted dressing gown lay an old gray sack. As Scraps held it up, she saw a note sticking out of the pocket. The Scissor Bird happened at that moment to be swinging on the chandelier so, snatching out the note, Scraps read it quickly herself and then passed it on to Peter.

"The Sandman's Nap Sack. Will put wearer to sleep at once," read Peter. Then, as Scraps put her finger warningly to her lips, he tucked the Nap Sack beneath his coat.

"We'll put 'em all to sleep," whispered Peter out of the corner of his mouth. "We'll send for Kuma's hand and get away from here!" They soon had a chance to try the Nap Sack, for Piecer and Scrapper, having some work to attend to in the garden, went out and locked the door in their usual manner.

Immediately Scraps threw down a pile of coats and stood up defiantly.

"I refuse to work any longer," she shouted, stamping her foot emphatically.

"Hah!" snapped the Scissor Bird, falling off the chandelier and stopping directly in front of Scraps' nose. "Every time you open your mouth you say something."

"Yes!" answered Scraps saucily, "and every time you say something you open your mouth." As the furious creature rushed at the Patchwork Girl, Peter threw the Nap Sack over his head. No sooner had he done so than its shrill voice grew lower and lower, until, with a tired flop, it fell to the floor and lay snoring like a zazagooch, which is the loudest snoring animal in Oz.

"We won't wait till night. We'll send the note now, Scraps," cried Peter triumphantly.

"What's up? What's up. Don't leave me," begged the little bear, crowding close to Peter. "I'm tired of being cross. I want to go some place where I can be pleasant without losing my position."

"All right! All right!" promised Peter. "But you'll have to help us, Grumpy. Now keep quiet while I write to Kuma." Pulling out the crumpled letter, Peter found a pencil and scribbled on the bottom of the page: "We are prisoners in the palace of Patch. Please send us your hand to unlock the doors and help us to escape." Signing his name hurriedly, Peter tossed the note into the air. It disappeared almost at once and in high excitement the three sat down to await developments. "I believe we could take that Nap Sack off and use it again," observed Peter after a little silence.

"He might wake up," objected Scraps.

"But we can easily put him to sleep again." Tiptoeing over to the Scissor Bird, he took off the Nap Sack. As he did there was a crash outside and, hurrying to the window, they saw Kuma's right arm and hand smashing its way through the glass in the castle door.

"Hurry! Hurry!" cried Scraps. Tearing the work basket from her head she threw it into a corner and flung the crown jewels of Patch after it. "I abdicate!" chuckled the Patchwork Girl, turning expectantly toward the door.

"Now then," breathed Peter, "let's all stand together and run like sixty."

"If we stand, how can we run?" mumbled Grumpy, but no one answered the little bear, for at that instant the key turned in the lock, the door opened and in swept the arm of Kuma,

a stout club grasped in its hand. Motioning for them to follow, it whizzed down the hallway. Scrapper, running in from the garden to see what was happening, received a smart blow on the head. Piecer, panting up the steps from the kitchen, was picked up bodily and dropped out of the window.

Through the castle door, down the steps and out of the garden rushed the three adventurers. As they started down the road, a crowd of Quilty men, on their way to the palace with a fresh load of patches, stared at them in astonishment. Then, suddenly realizing that the Queen was escaping, they rushed after her with yells and shouts of disapproval. But the arm of Kuma laid about with the club, seeming to be everywhere at once, and with groans and screams the Quilties fell back. Only three of the bolder ones continued the chase. Over the most persistent of their pursuers Peter flung the Nap Sack and, as he fell snoring by the roadside, Grumpy sent the second flying into a ditch. Kuma's club soon disposed of the third and without further interruption they pelted down the crossroads of Patch.

Always Kuma's hand flashed on ahead, making the way easy, taking down fence bars, opening gates, thrusting aside the branches of trees. Many of the Quilties saw them from the cottage windows, but before they could get down to their doors the strange procession had passed by. Scraps, being magically made and stuffed with cotton, did not tire, but Grumpy and Peter were soon panting with exhaustion. There was a remedy for even this, however. Throwing down the club, Kuma's arm jerked first one and then the other into the air, carrying them by turns to the very edge of the little Kingdom.

In a small maple grove, several miles from Patch, they stopped to rest. Peter still had hold of Kuma's hand and would have liked to keep it longer, but gently disengaging itself, it patted him kindly on the shoulder, shook hands with Scraps and was gone. This time it left no note and regretfully they watched it soar over the tree tops and disappear from view.

"Well," gasped Peter, leaning back against a tree, "we're out of Patch and where do we go now, Scraps?"

"South by east, and if I'm right,
We'll reach the capital tonight!"

answered the Patchwork Girl cheerfully.

"Oh, I hope we do," puffed Peter, taking a long breath. "Come on, let's start, I'm rested."

"Do you realize that the Kingdom of Patch will go to pieces in four days without you?" grunted the little bear, pattering along beside Scraps.

"Let it!" cried Scraps, recklessly turning a cartwheel.

"I'll not be Queen and work all day,
I'm the Patchwork Girl of Oz, hurray!"

Scraps Meets Sultan of Suds

CHAPTER 11

WALKING slowly at first, and then more briskly, Peter and his companions hurried on in the direction Scraps had pointed out. Grumpy was very helpful, for whenever they were in doubt, the little bear would climb a tree and, after looking all around, would guide them to the best and widest of the roads that ran hither and thither through the pleasant land of the Winkies. After his last climb, Grumpy had reported a village ahead and, quite cheerfully, they trudged along under the banana trees that edged the roadway.

"Even if Ruggedo has reached the Emerald City," remarked Scraps, waving to a Winkie farmer at work in the fields, "we'll find some way to capture him. Our wizard is very clever, boys. Perhaps he has captured him already!"

"But with the magic cloak, Ruggedo will be invisible," answered Peter gravely, "all but the patch, and no one will know that he is there. I hope he's still in Zamagoochie. Do you think Ozma will be able to send me back to Philadelphia, Scraps?"

"Of course!" chuckled the Patchwork Girl, skipping at the mere mention of the little Queen. "Ozma can do anything."

"Well, I hope she sends me back in time for the game," sighed Peter. "It's only three days off and I'm pitcher. And I wish I could take Grumpy back for a mascot. Would you like to be our mascot, Grumpy?"

"It doesn't sound safe," mumbled Grumpy, wiggling his nose very fast. "What is a mascot, Peter?"

"Oh, a kind of pet to bring one luck," explained the little boy. "You could come to all the games and have all the cake and peanuts you wanted." Grumpy considered the matter for a few moments, then, dropping on all fours, shook his head.

"I belong to Scraps," he announced, looking up admiringly at the Patchwork Girl. "I'm her pet. Besides, I'll never leave Oz."

"Why not?" asked Peter in surprise.

"Oh, because—" Rearing up on his hind legs, Grumpy waved his paw solemnly. "In your country, Peter, I could only be a bear, but in Oz, I'm a bear and a person, too. That's why it's more fun to be an animal in Oz than a person. Look at me," he exclaimed complacently. "I can do everything a boy can do and everything a bear can do, so, of course, I have twice as much fun! Can you do this, for instance?" Drawing himself up into a ball, Grumpy started rolling down a grassy slope at the side of the road.

"Ho! Ho!" laughed Scraps, running after Grumpy, "he has you there, Peter."

"Yes, but we shouldn't have turned off the road," objected Peter, hurrying after the Patchwork Girl. "Stop! Scraps, stop!"

From a gentle slope, the hillside dropped suddenly downward and now none of them could stop. Faster and faster rolled Grumpy, faster and faster ran Scraps and Peter, catching at trees and bushes to keep from falling. Instead of grass, the ground beneath their feet grew smooth and slippery as ice and from an incline the hill turned to a regular mountain side. It reminded Peter of the time he had tried skiing and, after several frantic attempts to keep his balance, he fell flat on his face and finished the slide on his stomach. Scraps, too, after a few wild spins and flourishes, sat down hard and, in a state of breathless surprise, they reached the foot of the mountain. Grumpy had travelled most of the way on his ear and was growling terribly in his own language. He was covered with a fine yellow powder and, as Scraps and Peter slid past, he began to lick his fur furiously. But one taste was enough.

"Soap!" coughed the little bear, wrinkling up his nose. "Yellow soap, too!"

"No wonder it was so slippery," said Peter slowly. "Now how are we going to climb up again?"

"We're not!" announced Scraps, rising to her feet with great difficulty. "Might as well try to walk up a looking glass. Why, what funny trees!"

"They're rubber," announced Grumpy, giving himself a shake, "and every branch is a spray."

"A bath spray," marveled Peter, staring up at the snakelike mass of tubes overhead. They had landed directly under one of the rubber trees and, as Peter spoke, from every spray a perfect shower of warm water sprinkled down upon them. Covered with soap from their slide down the mountain, they were soon in a fine lather, especially the little bear. When they tried to dash out from under the rubber tree,

they immediately slipped and fell, for the ground was green soap and even more slippery than Soap Mountain. Spluttering with surprise and shock, they finally crawled on their hands and knees out of the tree's range.

"Water!" groaned Scraps dolefully.

> "Water makes my spirits sink,
> It's very bad for me, I think,
> I know I'll fade, perhaps I'll shrink."

"Don't shrink," begged Peter in alarm. "Shake yourself, old girl." Balancing herself with difficulty, the Patchwork Girl began shaking herself vigorously and wringing out her skirts, while Peter, rubbing the soap from his own eyes, saw that they were in a strange and amazing village, where everything was soap. The houses were built of small, square cakes and the walks laid out in large blocks of green soap. Turkish towel trees edged all the avenues and, stepping cautiously to the nearest one, Peter picked a towel and wiped his dripping face. Grumpy soon followed his example. Then both went to help Scraps, who was feeling both damp and discouraged. They were fanning her briskly with dry towels, when a procession of villagers came skating down the main street.

"So that's how they manage it," whistled Peter, taking a few skating steps himself to see how it was done.

"More soap?" grumbled Grumpy. "Let's run!"

"No, let's wait and see what they have to say," whispered Peter.

The villagers were quite close by this time and Peter was amazed to see that they also were entirely made of soap. They wore turbans and robes of turkish toweling and, with their arms tucked comfortably in their flowing sleeves, came skating toward the travellers. Some of them were pink, some green, some white and others violet, and they were all about the size of ten-year-old children.

"Hello!" said Peter politely, as the first soapman came to an abrupt stop before him. "How do you do?"

"As I please, mostly," retorted the soapman shortly, "but I'm afraid you won't do at all. Who cut you out, anyway?"

"Oh, fall down!" advised Grumpy, picking up his towel and beginning to fan Scraps again. "Fall down, why don't you?"

"Who are you?" sniffed the Patchwork Girl, wringing her hands. They were still full of water.

"We are Suds," answered the villager proudly. "But we will have to take you to the Sultan. Are you hard or soft?" he asked, turning again to Peter.

"Hard!" cried the little boy, stamping his foot defiantly. He regretted this action almost immediately, for his heel, slipping on the soap sidewalk, threw him down on the back of his head. At this the Suds simply bubbled over with amusement and scorn. Then one Sud seized him by the left arm, another by the right, and started skating down the street. Looking over his shoulder, he saw that Scraps and Grumpy were being treated in the same sudden fashion. But soon he grew so interested in his surroundings that he almost forgot his indignation. The cottages of smooth green and pink soap were really charming. The gardens were full of soap-bubble bushes and vines and the bubbles, with their shining colors, sparkled and shimmered in the sunshine. Fountains of perfume filled the air with fragrance and, besides the turkish towel and rubber trees, there were bushes covered with snowy powder puffs. As they reached the stately green soap palace it began to snow and, catching one of the flakes on the back of his hand, Peter discovered it was a soap flake. Hurrying them through the soap stone gates, the Suds pounded upon the castle door. It was immediately opened by a tar soap slave in a yellow robe and turban.

"Take these interlopers to Shampoozle," said the Sud who had first spoken to Peter.

"Whoozle?" gasped the Patchwork Girl, shaking the soap flakes from her hair. No one deigned to answer her question, but at the Sud's command two more slaves appeared and, bowing out the villagers, closed the castle door.

"Follow me, interlopers," said the slave and, skimming expertly over the polished soap floor, he started down the royal hallway.

"I suppose we might as well," giggled Peter and, taking Grumpy's paw, began sliding after the slave. The two other slaves slid gravely

behind and, as they reached two royal purple soap doors, the first slave threw up his arm and cried impressively:

"Give three salaams for the Sultan of Suds!" and, jerking open the door, he fell flat upon his nose. It was so unexpected that Peter and Grumpy lost their balance and salaamed in spite of themselves, but the Patchwork Girl slid defiantly up to the throne itself.

"I don't give three slams for anyone!" announced Scraps, snapping her fingers under Shampoozle's nose. "Show us the way out of here."

"What!" snorted the Sultan, rising shakily

from his throne. "You refuse to salaam? Caka! Bara!" He clapped his hands sharply. "Salaam her!" At his command, the two slaves behind Scraps seized her arms and, forcing her downward, touched her cotton nose to the floor three times.

While Scraps was still choking and spluttering with rage, Peter and Grumpy regained their footing and stared curiously at Shampoozle. He was sitting on an ivory soap throne with red sponge cushions. He seemed to be made of green soap and his towel turban was twice as high as the turbans of the other Suds.

"That will teach you how to treat a Sultan," sniffed Shampoozle, shaking a finger severely at the Patchwork Girl.

"Sultan!" cried Scraps, giving Caka and Bara each a push. "You're not a Sultan, you're an Insultan."

Shampoozle's eyes grew round with displeasure and Peter and Grumpy had some difficulty to conceal their mirth.

"There, there!" said the Sultan testily, "don't be impertinent. Kindly answer my questions, so I can put you in your proper places. What kind of soap are you made of, hard or soft, laundry or tub—are you floaters or sinkers?"

"We're not soap at all," declared Peter indignantly. "I should think—"

"Tut! Tut!" interrupted Shampoozle loftily, "I *am* thinking. Don't talk so fast, we'll soon make good soap of you. Why, we can make

soap of anything, even rubbish," he finished proudly. "Caka! Bara! Just see how they lather."

Before Peter or the others had time to object, the two slaves, with three wet sponges, were rubbing vigorously at their cheeks.

"No lather at all," sighed Shampoozle in evident disappointment. "Never mind, I'll use you somehow. That creature," he pointed contemptuously at Grumpy, "that creature, flattened out and rolled down, will make an excellent bath mat. The rag girl can be ripped up into wash cloths and the boy boiled down to soap fat."

"Bath mat!" roared the little bear, putting back his ears. "Why, you can't make a bath mat out of me. Don't you know I'm a pet? You'd better not touch Scraps either, she's a Queen and Peter's a pitcher!"

"Pause!" commanded the Sultan, extending his arm wearily.

"I'll pause and claw you!" threatened Grumpy, doubling up his furry fists. "We're on our way to the Emerald City to save the Queen and you daren't stop us!" While Grumpy was saying, or rather growling all this, Peter had noticed an open window at the back of the throne room. Signaling to Scraps, he pushed

aside the soap slaves and, seizing Grumpy's paw, made a grand slide for freedom. Scraps reached the window first and recklessly jumped. Then Peter and Grumpy, without one look, jumped down after her. Fortunately, Scraps landed first so that the little bear and the little boy had something soft to fall upon. The drop from the window was nearly thirty feet and they looked around rather breathlessly.

"Did we hurt you?" asked Peter, hopping up quickly and pulling Grumpy to his feet.

"No!" puffed the Patchwork Girl, raising her head experimentally, "but I feel rather flat. Shake me up, boys, and then we'd better run." So Grumpy took one of her arms and Peter the other and they shook with all their might. Scrap's cotton stuffing was still damp from the rubber tree's shower and her face had a wrinkled and rough-dry look but, quite cheerfully, she patted herself into shape. They had fallen on a flat gray beach and, leaning down to examine the soil, Peter discovered it was sand soap. Without stopping to discover anything more, they started to run along the shore of a deep blue lake. As the waves broke on the shore, they frothed and foamed beautifully and dancing soap bubbles formed and floated over the waves. At any other time Peter would have liked to stop and admire the view but, fearing pursuit, they all ran along as fast as they could. Cliffs of soap stone rose steeply in places and there seemed no way to cross the lake nor to escape from the slippery clutches of the Sultan of Suds. Finally rounding a large cliff, they came to an abandoned soap building. White soap bricks were lying about in orderly piles and stacked against the building itself were several huge slabs of soap, evidently intended for doors. Picking up one of the soap bricks, Peter hurled it into the lake and, as it floated jauntily off, threw his cap into the air.

"I have it!" cried Peter gaily. "This soap floats. We'll drag one of the big pieces down to the edge of the lake and float across."

It was hard work, for the slab they chose was both thick and heavy, but at last, after much pulling, tugging, grunting and pushing, they managed to launch their queer raft. Peter and Grumpy carried Scraps out so she would not get wet again, then, climbing carefully aboard themselves, sat down on the slippery surface. Peter had sensibly brought along a long bar of green soap and, using this as a pole, he pushed the raft out into the current.

"Good-bye to Suds!" yelled Scraps, as they slipped smoothly over the blue waters of the lake,

> "Good-bye to soap and water, too,
> Shampoozle, you're a sham—shampooh!"

Friend Oztrich Offers to Help

CHAPTER 12

THEY were half way across the sudsy lake before any of the Suds themselves appeared. Then a whole company of them rushed down to the shore. Peter waved his cap cheerfully and, redoubling his efforts with the soap bar, pushed their raft toward the opposite bank.

"I'm afraid we've wasted a lot of time," puffed Peter, as the raft slid in toward the beach.

"Never mind," grinned Scraps, "we've something new to talk about. I'm glad we met the Suds, Peter."

"Humph!" sniffed Grumpy, balancing himself carefully. "I'm glad they met us. Now they'll have something new to talk about, something worth while." Peter chuckled a little at this and, seizing Scrap's hands, helped her to rise, for little waves were rippling aboard and he did not want the Patchwork Girl to fade or shrink.

But without any accidents or spills the raft washed up on the beach and they all jumped off.

"Do you think you still know which direction to take?" asked Peter anxiously.

"Which direction to take, which direction to take,
I lost my direction out there in the lake!
We'll have to start on and just trust to good luck;
What kind of a desert is this we have struck?"

Throwing up her arms, Scraps looked around in dismay.

"A wilderness!" quavered the little bear, sitting down resignedly on a tree stump. Shading his eyes, Peter stared off in the distance. As far as he could see, there was nothing but a barren stretch of desert, with here and there a tree or jagged rock.

"Let's start toward that tall pine," suggested Peter, pulling his cap down hard over his left eye and waving toward a pine tree just visible on the sky line. "If we keep walking we're bound to come out somewhere, but I'm afraid we'll never catch up with Ruggedo now."

"Maybe he's lost, too," said Grumpy, ambling along beside Scraps on all fours.

"Yes, but he has a magic cloak to help him," sighed Peter, "and all we have is an emerald we don't know how to work."

"Which tree are we walking toward?" asked Scraps, blinking her suspender button eyes rapidly. "I don't see any pine tree now, Peter."

"Neither do I," growled Grumpy, rising up on his hind legs, and neither did Peter when he looked again. As he strained his eyes for a glimpse of the missing tree, all the stumps and stones around them began to change places as naturally as if it were quite the usual thing to do, while the sand beneath their feet began to slip and slide uncomfortably.

"Wouldn't this make your hair curl?" Breathing hard, Grumpy edged closed to Scraps. As he did, a whole cluster of bushes jumped up and, seizing branches, danced madly about the three travellers.

"Here we go 'round the mulberry bush—mulberry bush—mulberry bush!" chanted Scraps, putting her hands up to her eyes.

"You mean, here they go 'round us!" mumbled Peter dizzily. "Stop! Stop! Go away, I never saw anything so silly."

The bushes, however, went gaily on with their dance, but when they had circled around the travellers at least a hundred times, they seemed to tire of the sport and all of them skipped off together.

"This makes me cross," growled Grumpy, scowling terribly.

"Well, it makes me cross-eyed," acknowledged Scraps, starting forward uncertainly. "Look out for that tree, Peter, it's going to trip you if it can. I'll tell you, let's shut our eyes and run!" Trying to walk straight ahead with trees, rocks and bushes jumping about like colts was certainly a problem and, closing their eyes, they did begin to run. But a young tree, dropping across their path, soon put a stop to that and they all fell sprawling together. Rubbing his knees, Peter sat up.

"Wish we had Kuma's hand to guide us through this place," muttered the little boy, brushing his hand wearily across his forehead.

"What we need is blinkers," sniffed Grumpy. "Hello, I see something that hasn't moved for a whole minute."

"Where?" Peter and Scraps spoke in the same breath. Swallowing hard, Grumpy waved his paw toward a great feathery bush, with three main branches. Without a word they kept their eyes fixed upon it for several minutes. Then Peter, jumping up determinedly and giving no heed to the skipping stones and slipping sands, ran straight for the bush. As fast as they could, Grumpy and the Patchwork Girl followed him. It was quite a distance and Scraps was tripped up several times on the way, but at last they stood before the only stationary object in that whole whirling wilderness.

"Feathers!" gasped Peter, pushing back his cap.

"And it's alive," cautioned Grumpy, moving back a few steps. "See, it has feet."

"It looks like—it may be—why, it *is!*" Rushing forward, Scraps tapped the strange creature smartly on the leg. Peter had supposed it had three legs and no head, but at the Patchwork Girl's tap, a head burst through the sandy soil and, rearing its long neck, an Oztrich looked at them inquiringly. Now an Oztrich, I don't mind telling you, is quite like an ostrich, except that it has green feathers and blue eyes.

"Well?" hissed the oztrich, looking sadly from one to the other. "Where do you think you're going?"

"That's what we want to know," cried Scraps, for Peter was too surprised to speak. "Where are we going, how do we get there and what is your name?"

"My name is Ozwold," answered the great bird gently. "How do you feel?"

"Dizzy!" groaned Grumpy weakly.

"Bewildered," sighed Scraps, jumping aside to let three rocks roll by.

"I thought so." The Oztrich shook its head in a satisfied manner. "This is a Bewilderness, you know. Bury your heads like I do," he advised calmly.

"But we want to go to the Emerald City," put in Peter, "and if we bury our heads we'd smother. Couldn't you carry us to the Emerald City on your back?" he asked daringly.

"Oh, Ozzy, if you only would!" Clasping her hands, Scraps rolled her suspender button eyes pleadingly at the huge bird.

"Who'd take care of my child?" objected the Oztrich, blinking its eyes very fast and indicating with its bill an enormous egg lying beside it in the sand.

"Haven't you a wife?" asked Peter in surprise.

"She's gone home to visit her mother," explained the Oztrich in an embarrassed tone. "I must stay here till the egg hatches."

"Couldn't we take it with us?" proposed Peter eagerly. "Think how proud you'd be to have your child hatch out in the capital!"

"Ozma would give it a hatchday present, too," added Scraps coaxingly.

"If you stay here, a rock will probably rush by and break it to pieces. It's a wonder to me it hasn't been broken long ago," sniffed Grumpy, leaning over to touch the egg with his paw.

"Great moguls! I never thought of that!" Shifting from one foot to the other, the oztrich looked nervously down at his child. "If you carry my egg I *will* go away from here," he murmured in a troubled voice. "Might as well go to the Emerald City. I've always wanted to see the capital. Just wait though, till I get my bearings!" Burying his head in the sand again, the oztrich stood perfectly motionless for nearly ten minutes. Fidgeting with impatience and dodging trees and rocks as best they could, Peter and his companions waited anxiously for the head to reappear. It came up so suddenly, when it did come, that Grumpy fell over backward.

"Don't speak," warned Ozwold in a tense voice. "Don't speak or I'm lost. Climb up and we'll start at once!"

Scraps, taking a running jump, landed safely on the oztrich's back. Then Peter carefully handed up the egg and, boosted by the little bear, took his place behind Scraps. Grumpy himself climbed aloft with no difficulty and before they were fairly settled the oztrich began pounding across the Bewilderness. It missed all the trees and rocks very cleverly and, as it travelled nearly a mile a minute, conversation was out of the question. Scraps, for greater security, wound her long arms about its neck, Peter had his arms 'round Scrap's waist, the egg balanced carefully in his lap and Grumpy, blinking and gasping, bounced up and down behind Peter.

"I hope it knows where it's going," thought Peter, as the wind whistled through his hair and the desert sand stung his cheeks and eyelids. For almost a half hour the oztrich rushed along like an express, then changing its gait began to travel more slowly. They had come to the end of the Bewilderness by now and Peter was relieved to see again the yellow farms and fields of the Winkies.

"I've thought of something!" exclaimed Peter, leaning forward to whisper in the Patchwork Girl's ear. "If Ruggedo is afraid of hen's eggs wouldn't an oztrich egg frighten him much more?"

"Hurrah! Hurray, well I should say!" Squirming round, Scraps looked delightedly at the huge egg in Peter's lap. "As soon as you see Ruggedo, throw it at his head," advised Scraps, in an excited whisper.

"But I promised to keep it safe for the oztrich," objected Peter uneasily, "and I can't break my promise, can I?"

"You'd be breaking the egg, not your promise," said Scraps earnestly. "Besides, Ozma's more important than an oztrich egg."

"I'll threaten to throw it," decided Peter. "Anyway, we'll wait till we come to the Emerald City. Hello, what's this?" Looming up ahead was a high yellow wall. With a snort of displeasure, the oztrich came to a halt.

"Do you see any gate?" he wheezed, curling his long neck around at Peter.

"I see something over there to the right," answered the little boy, "But are you sure this is a safe place to go through?"

"No," admitted the Oztrich hoarsely, "but unless we go through, how are we to go on to the Emerald City?"

"I'll open the gate," volunteered Scraps, slipping easily to the ground. Running over to the right, Scraps soon found the hollowed out space Peter had noticed, but instead of a gate, an upright piano was wedged into the opening. Scraps tried to see over the top, but it was too tall. Then she tried to shove it aside, but it was too heavy. So shrugging her shoulders and tossing back her yarn, Scraps sat down at the piano and started to play the Grand March of Oz, which she had been practicing faithfully on Dorothy's piano back at the palace. At the first chord, the piano, as if moved on an invisible hinge, fell backwards and Scraps, taken entirely by surprise, jumped over the top. The oztrich was not slow to follow and he had barely jumped over the fallen piano before it snapped back into its upright position, shutting them into the queerest city Peter had yet seen.

CHAPTER 13

"NOW how did this happen!" Sitting exactly where she had fallen, Scraps folded her arms dramatically.

"Opening chords!" boomed a deep voice, and out from a niche in the wall sprang a handsome person in a bandmaster's uniform. "The gates of Tune Town are locked with piano keys," he explained graciously, "so when you struck the opening chords, of course you fell in."

"Very good," murmured Ozwold. "But now that we are in, how do we get out?"

"Out of tune?" exclaimed the bandmaster in a shocked voice. "Don't get out of tune, I beg of you, besides it's against the law. May I call your attention to our principle laws here?"

Raising his baton he pointed to a large poster on the wall and much to his astonishment, Peter read:

"No talking allowed, sing!
No walking permitted, dance!"

"But you're talking," said Peter, shifting the oztrich egg from one knee to the other.

"Ah, but this is the intermission. In a moment the music will begin and you must keep time, keep step and keep moving. We do everything to music here. Quick now, which would you rather do, sing and dance or play in the band? That bear ought to be in the band, he has such bandy legs! Would you care to be in the band, creature?"

Grumpy slid down from the oztrich and shook his head bashfully. "Let's stick together," he rumbled under his breath to Peter. "Tell him we're a quartet."

"This is very awk," sighed Ozwold, who always clipped off his words when he was annoyed. "I am a bird but I cannot sing a single note."

"Then keep quiet and dance," advised the bandmaster.

"But look here!" put in Peter impatiently. "We don't want to sing and dance, we just want to go through your town. We're in an awful hurry and haven't time to be in a show."

"Say 'Ah!' " commanded the bandmaster, giving no attention to Peter's remarks. Striking a tuning fork on a railing before him, he waited expectantly for them to begin. Raising one eyebrow Peter looked at Scraps and as Scraps,

jumping to her feet, winked her suspender button eyes, they both burst into a loud "ah," Grumpy and Ozwold joining in so vigorously that the bandmaster's cap blew off.

"That's fine," he approved, picking his cap up somewhat nervously. "And now you're in tune. When the music starts go where you wish, do what you want, but be sure to keep step and remember to sing, not to speak, or you will be arrested."

"Oompah! Oompah! Who are these strangers?" Dancing down the marble street came a small bobbed-haired Queen, with a very short skirt and a tunic embroidered all over with fiddles and horns. On her head for a crown was a hollowed out drum and by her side was a tom-tom cat, clattering and clanging as he ran along.

"Travellers, my dear Jazzma," answered the

bandmaster with a bow. As the Queen stared curiously at the travellers and they as curiously stared back, the loud roll of a drum sounded in the distance. Instantly from every dwelling marched men arrayed in gay uniforms like Oompahs and Tunesters in embroidered tunics like the Queen's, only instead of drums, on their heads they wore bright bandannas.

"It's a play!" murmured Peter, as Oompah placed himself hastily at the head of the band and all the Tunesters stood waiting with toes stiffly pointed. When Oompah raised his baton, the band burst into a lively march and the whole population began dancing in every direction. Some of the women and girls danced toward the markets, singing out their orders in rhyme, others began sweeping the pavements, carrying on long conversations in song as they swept. Everybody was doing something and doing it to music. It really was quite gay and, fluttering his plumes importantly, the oztrich began strutting along in perfect time to the music. Grumpy watching the Queen, who was just ahead, slid and shuffled along skillfully. As for Scraps, she simply outdid herself. Peter, from his vantage point on the oztrich's back, watched the whole performance with great interest, feeling exactly as if he were in a circus parade. The inhabitants of Tune Town seemed all to live in flats and the walls of their dwellings were covered with lines, notes and scales, while all the streets were marked with musical signs. The trees, instead of leaves, bore musical notes and when the wind swept through them played silvery tunes that mixed not unpleasantly with the music of the band. Song birds fluttered in the branches and, quite forgetting the law against speaking, Peter called out to Grumpy to look at them.

"If you have a word to say,
Sing it out in rhyme;
Do you wish to spoil our play
And throw us out of time?"

warbled the Queen, waving a drum stick at Peter. Peter grew very red and while he was trying to think up a rhymed reply the music started again and Scraps, capering up to Jazzma, chanted gaily:

"You really are a funny nation,
And must we sing our conversation?"

The Queen, taking three steps to the right and four to the left, nodded vigorously and, looking admiringly at the Patchwork Girl, sang:

"Maiden stay, you are so gay,
I'd like to look at you all day.
My maid in waiting you shall be
And live in rag time harmonee!"

Peter waited anxiously for Scraps to answer. Tune Town was so jolly, he was almost afraid Scraps would forget their important mission. But Scraps, for all her giddiness, was deeply attached to Ozma and extremely worried about the plans of Ruggedo for her downfall. So kicking up her heels, she sang out saucily:

"And that your Majesty would mean
To dance attendance on a Queen;
A maid of waiting, not for me,
  I'm the Patchwork Girl,
But I won't work, wheee!"

Turning a cartwheel, Scraps walked a few paces on her hands, then coming right side up, danced amiably along beside Jazzma. Peter chuckled to himself and hoped he would remember all of this nonsense to tell his grandfather. Then, suddenly catching sight of a small inn, set back among the tune trees, he reached over and touched Scraps on the shoulder. He was terribly hungry, but not being quick at rhymes could not put his hunger into song. Scraps, however, caught his meaning at once and again turned to address the Queen.

She had to sing quite loud for all the Tunesters were warbling about this and that till the confusion was terrible.

"If we stopped at this inn, would you think
us rude?
Your Majesty, my friends crave food!"

bawled Scraps not untunefully.

The Queen, who was dancing a fox trot and purchasing a bouquet from a flower girl at the same time, nodded graciously and screamed back:

"Eat if you wish, our Viol Inn
Is kept by the famous Daddy Linn,
But eat in time and use your feet,
Be careful not to drop a beat!"

Scraps sang back to Queen Jazzma:

"Using one's feet to eat's a feat
We've never tried, nor dropped a beat."

"If anyone drops a beat, I'll eat it," mumbled Grumpy under his breath. Fortunately no one heard him, and in a few moments they reached the inn. Pausing at the foot of the steps and still marking time to the music, they stared up with great interest. As they did so an old gentleman with a fiddle body and bow legs came skipping out on the porch.

"Before you eat, you must pay me
In harmonee, sweet harmonee!"

sang the Inn Keeper, accompanying himself upon his fiddle body with one bow leg, while he stood upon the other.

"Does he mean we have to sing?" whispered Peter, sliding off the oztrich and setting the egg down carefully under a tree. Scraps nodded and while Grumpy and the oztrich rolled their eyes at her pleadingly, she clasped her cotton hands and sang with great feeling a song she had made up about Sir Hokus, the Good Knight of Oz.

"As brave as a lion, as bold as a King,
Is Sir Hokus of Pokes; he can fight, he can sing,
He can sweep out the castle, but Hokus likes best
To bag a big giant, or go on a quest,
And in Oz an adventure is happening each minute
And whenever one happens, he's sure to be in it!"

"Well, he's not in this one," thought Peter almost as interested in Scrap's song as the Inn Keeper. As Daddy Linn was now bowing and smiling and motioning for them to come up, they started quite cheerfully up the steps. But no sooner had they set foot upon the first one than the whole flight danced off. You see, they were dance steps, all the steps in Tune Town are, but after dancing three polkas and a three-step, they waltzed back to the porch and somewhat dizzily the travellers jumped off.

"Let's run away, let's run away,
I can't keep dancing here all day,"

puffed Ozwold, proud to have made up a song at last.

"Eeney meeney miney mo, first you eat and then you go," answered Scraps. Peter and Grumpy quite agreed with her and, shuffling their feet in time to the music, they waited impatiently for the Inn Keeper to reappear. When he did come out he had four leather music rolls on a tray and handed them around as if they were the most delicious morsels imaginable.

"Fie! Fie! Have you no pie!" sang Scraps, while Peter and Grumpy shook their heads in disappointment.

Ozwold pecked savagely at onc of the rolls, but even he could not eat leather.

> "Pie? I have a grand piana,
> How would that suit, Miss Diana?"

The Inn Keeper looked inquiringly at the Patchwork Girl and, when she shook her head, danced crossly into the inn and slammed the door.

> "No wonder they call this a Viol Inn,
> No dinner at all, just a dreadful din!"

mumbled Scraps, who hated to have Peter disappointed. Peter, with a sigh, jumped over the flighty dance steps, picked up the oztrich egg and, with Grumpy shuffling disconsolately after, started back toward the main street.

"Very awk—when one can't talk," wheezed the oztrich, rolling its eyes sadly at Peter.

"Never mind, a way I'll find,
Tunester, will you be so kind—"

Touching a Tunester on the sleeve, Scraps trilled earnestly:

"Mister, will you show us how
To leave this town? We're going now."

"To get out of Tune, get out of Tune!
You'll find yourselves out, pretty soon,"

chuckled the singer, waltzing away unconcernedly.

"What do you suppose he means by that?" exclaimed Peter, forgetting that he was breaking the law again. No sooner had he spoken than the music and dancing stopped and this time the whole band rushed toward him with instruments threateningly upraised.

"Scream!" puffed the Patchwork Girl, struck by a sudden idea. "Altogether now, Ah!" Not knowing what else to do, Peter, Grumpy and the Oztrich screamed "Ah" as loudly as they could, Scraps joining in with a will. As each one screamed in a different key, the result was a perfectly dreadful discord. Covering their ears and dropping their horns and drums, the members of the band, Jazzma and her Tunesters fled in every direction. Before the last echoes of that "Ah!" had died away, the four offenders found themselves out of Tune indeed, though how they had gotten over the wall not one of them could have told you.

"Did we blow over?" asked Peter, looking down anxiously at the oztrich egg to see if it was broken.

"No," giggled Scraps, throwing a kiss in the direction of the wall, "we sang out of tune, Peter, and here we are out of Tune. Which road shall we take, boys?" There were three roads leading away from Tune Town and after quite a debate they chose the center one.

"I hope we find something to eat soon," sighed Peter, as Ozwold started briskly down the road. "I'm hungry as a bear!"

"Not as this bear," growled Grumpy, patting his middle sorrowfully.

Ozwold and His Friends Rush On

CHAPTER 14

"THAT was a fine place for you, Scraps," chuckled Peter as the oztrich thudded good humoredly along the sunny road. "You'd rather sing than talk anyway. But singing and dancing all your life, whew! How would you play base ball to music, I wonder. Imagine singing out signals and trying to make a home run to a waltz."

"The dinners were the saddest," sighed Grumpy, licking his chops hungrily. "Do you see any biscuit bushes or carrot trees around here?"

"There's some kind of a tree in that field," answered Peter, but the fruit is up so high we couldn't reach it, anyway."

"I could," grunted the little bear eagerly. "Let's stop and try." The oztrich had spied some especially appetizing rocks by the roadside and was quite willing to stop. So Peter placed his egg child beside him and, while they ran off to investigate the fruit tree, Ozwold lunched quite contentedly on a couple of cobblestones. The tree was about as tall as a cocoanut palm and clustered at the top were large green fruits about the size of watermelons.

Requiring no luncheon, Scraps danced off to amuse herself and, as Peter and Grumpy blinked hungrily upward, two of the melons detached themselves from the branch of the tree and came sailing gracefully downward.

"Why, they've umbrellas over them," gasped Peter.

"Of course," said the little bear calmly. "Have you never seen an umbrella melon?" Peter never had and said so quite frankly.

"Well," explained Grumpy, placing himself in a position to catch the larger of the two. "If they didn't have these umbrella attachments they'd smash to pieces when they fell. As it is,

when the fruit is ripe the umbrella leaves open and float them safely down. Ah-hh!" Holding out both arms, Grumpy neatly caught his melon and, hugging it blissfully, sat down to enjoy his first meal since leaving Patch. Peter had to chase his luncheon all around the field, for the breeze was brisk and the umbrella attachment larger than the melon itself. But finally he did manage to overtake it and bringing the melon back, settled down beside Grumpy. Cutting off the umbrella leaves with his pen knife, Peter split the melon in two. It was something like a cantaloupe, only much larger and much sweeter and to the tired, hungry, dusty little traveller, it tasted perfectly delicious. But, hungry as he was, half the melon was all he could eat and he looked in admiring astonishment as Grumpy burrowed his nose deeper and deeper into his. The entire center was gone and he was nibbling at the rind when Scraps came hurrying back across the field.

"Are you boys going to eat all day?
Glad I don't waste *my* time that way!"

"You don't know what you miss, Miss." Licking his nose, Grumpy grinned up at the Patchwork Girl, but Scraps, sticking out her tongue, merely turned a cartwheel, jumped over a fence, and landed neatly on the back of Ozwold. Peter and Grumpy were not slow to follow, for they were all anxious to reach the capital before nightfall.

"Is my child safe?" mumbled Ozwold as well

as he could with the two cobblestones still sticking in his throat. "Whatever you do, don't drop my child. He is my wife's favorite egg. I do hope he doesn't hatch out before we reach the Emerald City!"

"So do I," breathed Peter, looking quite nervously at the huge egg in his lap. "Have you ever been in the Emerald City?" he asked politely.

"No," answered the oztrich slowly. "Have you?" Peter shook his head and as Ozwold jogged along the lane, Scraps told him all about the capital of Oz and the delightful people who live there, ending up with the story of Ruggedo's escape and his wicked plan to steal all the Oz magic and make himself ruler of the realm.

"Ruler of Oz!" screamed the oztrich, stopping in consternation. "Great grandmothers, why didn't you tell me this before? Why, if that old gnome has a flying cloak, he's probably reached the Emerald City and captured everybody by this time. A gnome on the throne of Oz, how perfectly impos! Ruggedo ruler of Oz, how simply ridick!" At each word Ozwold grew more indignant, and finally, with a screech like an engine whistle, he hurled himself forward, running along at such speed that trees, fences, farms and hills whirled by in a blur of dust and Peter and the others had all they could do to keep their places. Hugging the oztrich egg with one arm and Scraps with the other, Peter blinked and bounced and tried to catch a glimpse of the country they were passing or the country they were coming to. But between the speed and the dust, he could see nothing.

"If he's just going in the right direction," thought the little boy, closing his eyes and gritting his teeth to keep them from chattering, "we'll get there in no time. If he isn't—"

"Whoa! Whoa!" roared Grumpy, as long as he had breath enough to roar. Even Scraps tried to check the mad plunge of their excited steed. But finally they all stopped shouting and devoted all their energies to hanging on. Peter rather expected they would run into something and so was not greatly surprised to find himself sitting in the middle of the road. Scraps sprawled beside him and Grumpy, rubbing his head, limped crossly out of a ditch. Ozwold himself was leaning up against a tree with both eyes closed, while across the roadway lay an extremely upset and odd looking traveller.

"I told you to whoa," growled Grumpy, shaking his paw angrily. "Now see what you've done!"

"Never say whoa to an oztrich," muttered the green bird, opening one eye. "Say whum!"

"But we've run over somebody," exclaimed Peter.

"Is my child broken?" asked the oztrich, opening the other eye and peering wildly in every direction. Fortunately the egg had fallen on a heap of soft sand and while Ozwold hurried over to assure himself it was not cracked, Scraps and Peter ran to help the stranger.

"Are you broken, stunned or killed,
Wrecked or sprained or simply spilled?"

quavered the Patchwork Girl, leaning over him.

"It's all right," sighed the stranger, sitting up slowly. "I'm used to being slammed. Just so my back's not broken, I don't care!"

"Why, it's a book!" burst out Peter, coming closer to make sure.

"Not a book, a bookman!" corrected the traveller, rising with Scrap's help to his feet. "Books are old fashioned, but a bookman is right up to date. I don't wait to be advertised, I speak for myself, I don't lie around waiting to be read, I run after people and make them read me. I can carry myself and turn over a new leaf every day in the year. I'm very interesting!" finished the bookman, with a wide smile at Peter. Peter smiled back and how could he help it? Above his big book body the fellow had a round jolly face with floppy dog ears. His legs and arms were quite thin and he was about as tall as Scraps.

"Are you sure you're not hurt?" asked the little boy, as the bookman began to run briskly up and down thumping the covers of his book body to knock out the dust.

"What are you about?" asked Grumpy, looking curiously at the traveller and still rubbing his head with his paw. "Have you any animal tales?"

"Or verse?" cried the Patchwork Girl eagerly.

"Or baseball stories?" questioned Peter, coming closer and closer. In their interest they had almost forgotten the oztrich.

"I've all kinds of stories," boasted the bookman and, unclasping his middle, spread wide the pages of his book. "Which will you have first?"

"A bear story," said Grumpy, sitting down on his haunches and waving both paws. "Bear stories are the most exciting!"

"No, a verse," shrilled the Patchwork Girl quickly. Peter was about to call for a baseball story when he suddenly remembered his manners.

"Ladies first," said Peter, looking reprovingly at the little bear. "Just show us one of your verses," he remarked carelessly.

"Funny or sad?" asked the bookman, running his finger down his table of contents.

"Funny, of course," chuckled Scraps, tossing her head impatiently. Turning his pages rapidly the bookman stepped off a few paces and, leaning forward, the three travellers read:

"Do fishes use the liquid tones
The world so highly praises?
Could they speak dryly, and do bees
Converse in honeyed phrases?"

"Ho! Ho!" laughed Peter merrily, "if they do they'd soon get stuck. That's a good one—almost as good as your verses, Scraps."

"There's a much funnier one on page seventy-six," said the bookman gaily. "Wait!"

"What for?" Coming up behind them, Ozwold looked severely at their new friend. "What are we waiting for?" he repeated sternly.

"This is the man you ran over," explained Peter quickly, "and he's letting us read his book."

"And you stand here reading with the whole Kingdom in danger?" hissed the oztrich, thrusting his long neck forward angrily. "A nice way to save the Queen, I must say."

"I've a chapter on saving, somewhere, but I'm afraid it's on saving money," mumbled the bookman, thumbing his pages over hurriedly. Peter and Scraps looked rather crestfallen and, while they walked slowly toward the oztrich, he again addressed the bookman.

"If you know so much, perhaps you can tell us the way to the Emerald City," he wheezed disagreeably.

"I'm not a guide book," answered the bookman stiffly.

"Then shut up," advised the oztrich so sharply that without intending to at all the bookman did shut up.

"Are you coming, or do I have to save the Kingdom myself?" asked the oztrich, turning impatiently to Peter.

"I'll come, too, and entertain you as you go along. Read as you run," said the bookman brightly.

"Not as I run," sniffed Ozwold, who seemed determined to snub this new acquaintance. "Better keep out of my way or you'll be run over again."

"I'm afraid you will," said Peter, patting the bookman kindly on the back, for he seemed quite crushed by Ozwold's rude speeches.

Scraps had already mounted the oztrich and now, leaning far out to the side, shook hands with the bookman, singing:

"Bookman! Bookman, don't you care,
We'll see you some day somewhere,
Come to the Emerald City, do
And then I'll read you through and through!"

"So will I," promised Grumpy earnestly. "You'll find us in the palace. Just ask for the Queen of the Quilties and her pet," finished the little bear grandly.

"There won't be any palace if you stand here much longer," fumed the oztrich, kicking up the dust angrily. *"Come on!"*

Realizing that there was some truth in the oztrich's remarks, Peter picked up the huge egg and climbed aboard. Grumpy, growling under his breath, took his seat behind Peter.

"This is no time for improving literature," hissed the oztrich, starting off at a two legged trot. Peter did not bother to answer, but waved his cap cheerily to the bookman, who still stood uncertainly in the middle of the road. He kept on waving till the bookman became a mere speck in the distance, then, turning about, devoted all his attention to holding on. For nearly an hour Ozwold pelted down the endless road. Then suddenly Scraps clutched him excitedly about the neck.

"Stop!" shouted the Patchwork Girl. "Stop! Stop!"

"What's the matter?" coughed the oztrich, slackening his speed a trifle.

> "Turn out between those pear trees quick,
> I see the road of yellow brick,"

cried Scraps, waving one arm joyfully over her head.

"Where does that take us?" inquired Peter, leaning curiously over Scraps' shoulder.

> "To the Emerald City's golden gate;
> Home! Home at last, I can hardly wait!"

sang Scraps, nearly choking the oztrich in her excitement. "Hurry, Ozzy, hurry! Hurry!"

"Don't forget to whum when you come to the Emerald City," grumbled Grumpy, as the great green bird gathered itself together for another burst of speed.

"The Emerald City may be destroyed for all we know," wheezed Ozwold gloomily. "But hold tight, everybody. Here we go!"

I II III IV V VI 7 8 9 10 11 12 OCLOCK

CHAPTER 15

THE Gilliken Country of Oz has always been a favorite retreat for witches, wizards and sorcerers. Since the practice of magic has been forbidden for everyone except Glinda, the Good Sorceress of the South, and the Wizard of Oz, a great many of the lesser wizards and magic workers have retired to the mountains of the north to practice in secret or study for their own satisfaction the ancient art of wizardry.

In a crystal cavern on the western slope of Zamagoochie lived Wumbo, the Wonder Worker. In his youth, Wumbo had studied in the best schools of sorcery and was not only an accomplished magician, but a lovable and loyal citizen of Oz. Therefore, when Ozma passed a law against the practice of magic, Wumbo withdrew to his favorite cave and quietly and harmlessly continued his studies. Now, of all studies sorcery is the most profitable. Being able to grant most of his own wishes, Wumbo lived in the utmost comfort and contentment, his cavern being almost as magnificent and luxurious as Ozma's castle. From preference, Wumbo lived by himself, but was seldom lonely, for when you can conjure up a company of acrobats from a handful of pebbles, or an orchestra from a few sticks and dried peas, you are always sure of entertainment. Long after ordinary Oz folk were in their beds, Wumbo, in his crystal study, would pore over his musty books of magic, trying out new spells and charms for his own satisfaction and amusement.

He was especially fond of his book of Chants and Enchantments and, on the evening I am writing of, sat beside his great crystal lamp, turning over its leaves and humming cheerfully to himself.

"I think," mused Wumbo at last, "I shall use the speech-giving chant, tonight. It's been a long time since I've talked with my furniture and no doubt it has a lot to tell me!" Rubbing his hands gleefully, Wumbo turned to page ninety-seven and, after reading the chant several times to himself, walked over to his foot-stool and, touching it gently, droned:

"Ooney, mooney, nooney nill,
Tell me foot-stool what you will."

"I need re-covering," creaked the foot-stool promptly. "And next time you trip over me, I trust you will crack both shins."

"Ho! Ho!" roared the wizard, bending backward and forward with mirth, "that's nice of you. Anything else?" As the foot-stool made no further remark, he walked to the mantel and touched the clock.

"Ooney, mooney, nooney nill,
Tell me, old clock, what you will."

"Your wig's on crooked," ticked the clock critically, "and there's a smudge on the end of your nose." Looking in the glass, Wumbo saw that the clock, as usual, was telling the truth.

Straightening his wig, he went next to his favorite chair.

> "Ooney, mooney, nooney nill,
> Tell me, arm-chair, what you will!"

chanted Wumbo, putting both hands in his pockets.

"Somebody's sitting on me," complained the chair in a stuffy voice.

"Somebody's sitting on you," gasped Wumbo in astonishment. "Why, I don't see anybody!"

"Then feel 'em," whispered the chair hoarsely. Putting out his hand cautiously, Wumbo touched a long wispy beard and immediately jumped back with a cry of alarm.

"Fold your arms! Fold your arms!" spluttered the Wonder Worker, rushing back to the Book of Enchantments. The chair lost no time in obeying this order. Instead of ordinary arms, Wumbo's chair had real ones and it clasped them about the invisible sitter, so that he could neither move, scream nor scarcely breathe. Meanwhile, with trembling fingers, Wumbo fluttered over the pages of the Chant Book, till he found the exact one he was searching for—the chant to render visible the invisible.

> "Ominey, hominey, dominey deer,
> I command you invisible one to appear!"

mumbled Wumbo, straightening his specs excitedly, for he had had no visitors for seven years. Instantly the figure of a gray gnome appeared in the armchair, kicking, struggling and sputtering with fright and fury. As Wumbo continued to stare at him, the chair lowered one of its arms, and Ruggedo, for, of course, it was the old Gnome King, jerked up his head and roared loudly:

"Take me to the Emerald City! Take me to the Emerald City!"

"Are you addressing me?" asked Wumbo, dropping into a chair opposite the gnome and regarding him attentively. "If you are, you may as well save your breath. I have never practiced long-distance magic and could not send you to the Emerald City, even if I wanted to."

"Who wants your old magic," sneered Ruggedo. "I've magic of my own. Take me to the Emerald City. Take me to the Emerald City!" he screeched, trying in vain to squirm out of the clutching arms of Wumbo's chair.

"You are evidently unfamiliar with one of the first and simplest of magic laws," observed the wizard reprovingly. "I see now that you are wearing an invisible cloak, but two magic charms cannot work at the same time and as I spoke first you will have to wait till my chant wears off."

"Who are you? Where am I? How dare you keep me here!" panted Ruggedo furiously.

"You are in the Zamagoochie Country, in the humble cave of Wumbo the Wonder Worker," answered the old gentleman quite amiably. "And as you came here yourself, why blame me for trying to entertain you as I see best?"

"I knew it! I knew it!" raged the Gnome King. "This is Peter's doing. When I catch that boy I'll turn him to a peach basket and jump on him! And you, I suppose, are the father of that meddling Kuma Party?"

"Why, yes," said Wumbo in surprise. "Have you met my son?" Ruggedo gave a spiteful nod, and began to struggle anew with the arms of the chair.

"I command you to let me go," puffed the Gnome King. "I've important business in the Emerald City and must reach there tonight."

"I'm afraid that will be impossible," sighed Wumbo softly. "When my chair takes a fancy to a person, it sometimes hangs on to him for days and days. Why not sit still and rest yourself," he suggested, folding his arms comfortably. Seeing that for the present he was perfectly powerless, Ruggedo lay back and glared at the old wizard, his red eyes snapping with rage and resentment.

"I'll report you to Ozma," threatened the Gnome King darkly. "You know perfectly well that you are breaking the law, having all this magic furniture and stuff."

"Take your feet off my rounds," ordered the chair sharply, giving Ruggedo a good squeeze.

"How about your magic cloak?" said Wumbo, smiling a little as Ruggedo hastened to take his heels off the rungs of the chair, "and how about turning a boy to a peach basket? That sounds like pretty bad magic to me. Who is this boy? And why are you wearing a cloak of invisibility?"

"That's my business," muttered the gnome, looking uneasily around. "Are you going to let me go or not?"

"That depends on where you are going and what you are going to do," answered Wumbo, clapping his hands three times. A box of chocolates instantly appeared and tilted invitingly toward the wizard. Helping himself, Wumbo offered a chocolate to Ruggedo, but the gnome shook his head impatiently, so Wumbo clapped his hands again and the chocolates disappeared.

"I am going to the Emerald City to report the discovery of a treasure ship," explained the Gnome King after a short silence. "I am going to have Ozma transport the jewels and gold pieces to her own castle. I'm making her a present of them," finished Ruggedo virtuously.

Wumbo said nothing but, rising slowly, went over and stared into a great crystal ball on his desk. "That, of course, is not true," said Wumbo, coming back to sit in his chair. "My crystal ball tells me that much and my own eyes tell me that you are wicked and untrustworthy. Therefore I shall keep you here until I find some way to warn Ozma of your coming."

At these words Ruggedo was simply beside himself. Kicking and screaming and threatening Wumbo with every sort of death and destruction, he writhed about in the chair. But Wumbo was not easily frightened and, picking up the Book of Enchantments, began to read it to himself, while the arm chair, indignant at the Gnome King's bounces and screeches, hugged him till he was forced to keep quiet. But sitting there in the firelight, he did a lot of thinking, and as it grew later and later and quieter and quieter in the great crystal cavern, the Gnome King's spirits began to rise. For Ruggedo was beginning to remember some of his magic.

"If he doesn't try any more chants, the present ones will wear off in four hours," thought the old gnome craftily. "Four hours, and then for the magic cloak!" Wumbo, himself, fully intended to keep a strict watch over his visitor, but the heat from the fire and the drowsy chants in the old book made him sleepier and sleepier. Besides, he had the utmost confidence in his arm-chair and, not realizing that Ruggedo knew the length of time the magic chants would take to run out, he felt sure the old gnome would not try again to use his cloak. So he read on and on and, while he was searching for the chant to force a person to tell the truth, the book slipped from his knees and a loud snore issued from his lips.

"Wake up, Master! Wake up!" buzzed the clock, tilting forward in alarm.

"Wake up! Wake up!" scolded the arm-chair and foot-stool both together. But before they could arouse the wizard, Ruggedo had vanished. Four hours had passed to the very minute, the magic of the wizard's chant had worn entirely away and at a whispered command from the Gnome King, the magic cloak had lifted him out of the imprisoning arms of Wumbo's chair and whirled him off and away. Over mountains, hills and valleys flew the gnome in his invisible cloak,

through the chilly mists of early morning till, far below, he saw the flashing spires of the Emerald City of Oz.

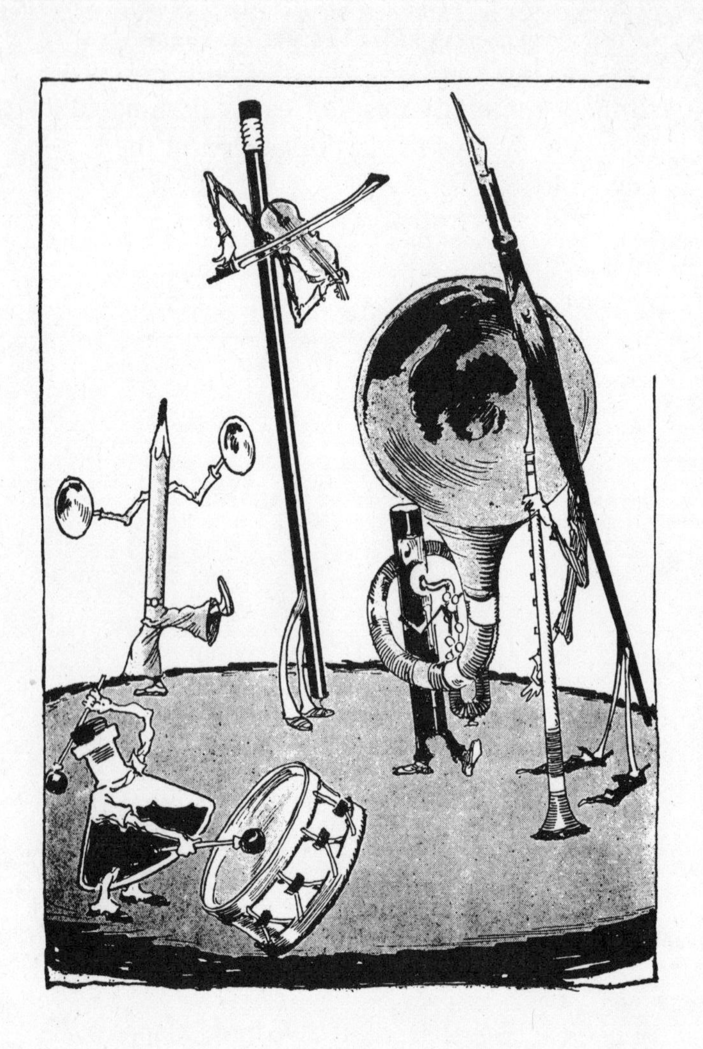

Kuma's Hand Is at Work Again

CHAPTER 16

AS the chair, foot-stool and clock lost their power of speech at the same instant the Gnome King regained his freedom, there was no one to arouse Wumbo. And it was nearly noon time before he did awaken. Puzzled to find himself in a chair instead of bed he straightened up, gave himself a shake and blinked sleepily up at the clock. Something about the clock reminded him of his bad little visitor and, whirling round, he stared anxiously at his arm-chair. But of course Ruggedo was not there.

"Gone!" exclaimed the wizard, clapping his hand to his head. "Wumbo, you're growing old and stupid. What's to be done now? What's to be done now?"

Shuffling anxiously up and down his crystal hearth, Wumbo tried to think of the quickest way to locate the wicked little gnome. A loud thump upon the door interrupted his wonderings and, as he mechanically muttered the magic phrase that opened it, the arm and hand of Kuma Party came flying into the study.

"A message from my son," breathed Wumbo, hurrying forward to clasp the hand. There was a note folded up in the palm and while the wizard opened it the arm settled quietly down beside the clock.

"Dear father," wrote Kuma, "a small mortal boy and a gnome came to my cottage yesterday afternoon. The boy is lost and the gnome quite evidently means mischief. Knowing the perils for a mortal boy traveling in a magic country, I offered to lend him my hand if he ever needed it. This morning he sent for help and I have dispatched my right arm and hand to help him escape from the Kingdom of Patch and am sending my left to you for instructions. Can you, by your magic, suggest a way to locate the gnome and keep the boy from harm?

"Your dutiful and affectionate son Kuma."

Pushing his specs high on his forehead and knocking his wig sideways, Wumbo dashed over to his desk, and wrote:

"Send your arm to the Emerald City. The gnome has gone there wearing a cloak of invisiblity. Take a letter of warning to Ozma and find and hold the gnome till Ozma can by her magic overpower him."

Folding the paper, he slipped it into Kuma's hand. The hand closed over it at once and in a flash the arm swept out of the cave and away over the Gilliken mountains.

"Well," sighed Wumbo, sinking into his chair, which immediately gave him a reassuring little hug, "that ought to help some. But the gnome certainly means to make trouble!"

Wumbo had never mastered long-distance magic and his spells and chants worked only when he was present, but feeling that he had done all that he could without breaking the law, and being fatigued by so much thinking before breakfast, he gently clapped his hands. In a flash an appetizing repast floated in on a golden tray and settled upon his desk. Pulling up his chair, Wumbo mumbled a few words over the pens and pencils scattered about his desk. Next instant they had rolled to the floor and straightened up into an orchestra of five pieces. Softly and sweetly they began to play an old Oz quadrille and, somewhat soothed and comforted, the Wonder Worker began eating his breakfast.

Mystery in the Emerald City

CHAPTER 17

"OF course," said Dorothy, leaning down to tie her gold slipper, "of course, Ozma has only been gone since yesterday, but even so, I think it would be fun to have a party to welcome her home."

"So do I! I love parties!" Clasping his knee with his clumsy, stuffed hand, the Scarecrow smiled down at the little girl. He had just walked over from his corn-ear residence and they were sitting cozily in a big swing on the front porch of the palace.

"Where did Ozma go?" asked the Scarecrow, taking off his hat and smoothing back the few wisps of straw that served him for hair.

"Just to spend the night with Glinda," said Dorothy, picking up a book of party games and beginning to flip over the pages. "Ozma has her magic belt with her and is going to wish herself back at three o'clock. Why, what are you laughing at?" Putting down the book, Dorothy stared reproachfully at her companion.

"I'm not laughing," said the Scarecrow solemnly, "but why pinch me that way? Of course, I have no feeling, but it's not very polite."

"I didn't pinch you at all," exclaimed Dorothy, sitting up very straight. The Scarecrow eyed the deep dent in his stuffed arm, looked suspiciously all round and then, seeing no one but Dorothy, moved quickly to the opposite end of the swing.

"What's the matter?" rumbled a deep voice and, coming out from behind a gold pillar, the Cowardly Lion paused before the royal swing. The Cowardly Lion had come to the Emerald City with Dorothy on her very first adventure and is the biggest pet in the palace. He was a bit out of breath, for he had just been running a race with his friend the Hungry Tiger. "What's the matter?" he panted anxiously, for Dorothy was frowning crossly and the Scarecrow, in spite of his painted smile, looked extremely sulky.

"While I was telling him about Ozma's party, he laughed at me," pouted the little girl, moving as far as she could from the straw man.

"But she pinched me," explained the Scarecrow in an injured voice, "for no reason whatever!" It was so unusual for these two—or for anyone in the Emerald City—to quarrel, that the Cowardly Lion could scarcely believe his lion ears and, when Dorothy began to protest angrily that she had not pinched the Scarecrow, he held up his paw pleadingly.

"Oh, let's talk about the party," begged the lion in a shocked roar. "What were you planning, my dear?"

"Well," said Dorothy, flashing an angry glance at the Scarecrow, "first I was going to have a speech of welcome, then games and dancing and, after that, Ozcream and—"

"Ouch!" coughed the lion, interrupting Dorothy with an angry growl. "Who pulled my tail?" Rolling his eyes from one to the other he rose to his feet, trembling in every knee. "I've known you nearly all my life," roared the Cowardly Lion, shaking his mane furiously, "but no one can pull my tail. Not even you, Dorothy."

"Oh dear! Oh dear! I think you're both perfectly horrid!" Throwing down her book, Dorothy jumped out of the swing, and dashed around the side porch, where she bumped violently into Sir Hokus, who was taking his morning turn on the veranda.

"Odds daggers!" ejaculated the Knight, straightening his shield and buckler. "What's wrong, maiden?"

"Everything!" wailed Dorothy, throwing her arms round his neck. "Just because I'm trying to plan a party everybody is fighting with me."

"Fighting?" puffed Sir Hokus, brightening up at the mere sound of the word, for he did dearly love a battle. "Well, I'm on your side. Who dares to fight with Princess Dot?" thundered the Knight in his deep voice and, seizing her hand, stepped quickly around the corner of the porch. But when he saw the Cowardly Lion and the Scarecrow simply glaring at one another, he paused in dismay. They were his oldest friends and never, since his arrival in the Emerald City, had he had a disagreement with either of them. Feeling that there must be some mistake, he strode hastily between the two celebrities and held up his hand. As he did, he received a staggering blow on the head that pushed his helmet well down over his ears.

"Odds dragons and flagons!" blustered the Knight, sputtering like a red hot coal. "Have at you, villains! Varlets! Rascals and rogues!" Drawing his sword, he began slashing in every direction, but as his helmet was over his eyes, he fortunately did no harm.

Crouching behind the swing, Ruggedo, in his invisible cloak, rocked to and fro with silent merriment, holding his sides and shaking all over with malicious glee. Arriving at the palace early that morning, the Gnome King had immediately ordered the cloak to carry him to the royal apartment. But Ozma, to his great disgust and disappointment, was not there. Neither was his belt, nor any of the little Queen's magic appliances, for she had taken them all with her to Glinda's castle. Until he had the belt, Ruggedo was perfectly powerless

and, after his first disappointment had worn off, he determined to wait for Ozma's return, seize the belt as soon as she appeared and at once destroy the Emerald City and all of its inhabitants.

While he waited, Ruggedo had run here and there about the palace, amusing himself in his own spiteful fashion. Now that he had learned from Dorothy the exact time of Ozma's return, he fluttered off to the kitchen to steal some breakfast and plague the cook. Meanwhile Sir Hokus had tripped over a flower pot and fallen flat, while the Cowardly Lion and the Scarcrow had retreated behind two porch pillars. Dorothy, terribly alarmed at the serious turn the quarrel had taken, rushed hurriedly forward. Now that Ruggedo had gone, the whole thing seemed silly and ridiculous.

"Let's make up," begged Dorothy, helping Sir Hokus to his feet. "I'm sure it's all a mistake."

"Well, it was a great mistake to pull my tail," rumbled the Cowardly Lion, coming out very slowly and majestically, "but I'll overlook it this once." He blinked suspiciously at the Scarecrow, but the Scarecrow was helping Sir Hokus with his helmet and did not even notice.

"Who thumpst me again—" panted the Knight, pointing his forefinger furiously downward—"who thumpst me again—d—dies!"

"But nobody will!" Dorothy hastened to assure him. She looked pleadingly at the Scarecrow, who she felt must be responsible. "Let's forget all about it and think about the party," she proposed brightly. "Now, who'll make the speech of welcome?"

"Let Scraps do it," muttered the Cowardly Lion, licking his paws sulkily. "She's clever at speeches and makes short ones, too. I'll go find her," he offered in a little more cheerful voice. "Haven't seen her since yesterday, but I s'pose she's around somewhere."

"All right," smiled Dorothy, as the Cowardly Lion thudded across the porch. "Now, who'll help me decorate the banquet hall?" Sir Hokus had taken off his helmet and was rubbing his head wrathfully. At Dorothy's words he glanced across at the Scarecrow, but the straw man's painted eyes met his so frankly and innocently that he impulsively put out his hand. Certainly the Scarecrow's flimsy arm could never have dealt him such a blow.

"We'll help you," said the Knight, taking the Scarecrow's arm. " 'Twas that villain lion who thumped me," he whispered as they started for the banquet hall.

"Here come Betsy and Trot," cried Dorothy, forgetting all about the quarrel. "Maybe they will pick some flowers for the table!"

Betsy and Trot, as many of you already know, are two little mortals like Dorothy, who have been invited by Ozma to live in the royal palace. Both reached Oz after ship-wrecks and many trying adventures and they found life in the capital so exciting and gay that they have never wished to return to the United States. They were delighted at the prospect of a party, and so was the Hungry Tiger, who had come up just behind them. Putting a huge flower basket on his back, the two little girls ran gaily down the palace steps.

"I'll have a strawberry sandwich," purred the tiger, looking over his shoulder at Dorothy. "Be sure to have strawberry sandwiches!"

"I never heard of a strawberry sandwich," laughed the little girl, shaking her head dubiously.

"Well, there always has to be a first," chuckled the tiger, trotting after Betsy.

Dorothy, looking a little puzzled, waved after him and, well pleased with her plans, ran into the castle to ask the Wizard of Oz to think up some new tricks to entertain the guests, and to confer with the cook about refreshment. Soon the palace began to hum with activity. The banquet hall, under the skillful hands of the Scarecrow and Sir Hokus took on a truly festive air. Messengers and pages ran hither and thither with invitations, while the Royal band, tuning up on the castle lawn, added its strains to the general gaiety. Indeed, from the preparations for her return, one would have thought Ozma had been gone a year instead of a day, and Ruggedo, fluttering here and there in his invisible robe, chuckled with amusement and malice.

"Work away," muttered the Gnome King darkly. "At three o'clock I shall send you all to the bottom of the Nonestic Ocean, transport my gnomes here and enjoy this party my own self." At first, Ruggedo had continued his pinchings and punchings and hair pullings but, at last, fearing detection, he had stopped his mischievous teasing and seated himself calmly in Ozma's chair at the head of the banquet table. In this position it would be a simple matter to unclasp his magic belt as soon as the little fairy made ready to take her place. The patch, which was the only visible thing about Ruggedo, was now on the seat of the chair, so did not show and, quite unconscious of their dreadful peril, Dorothy and her friends went on with their preparations for the party, while

Ruggedo, fidgeting with impatience, kept his eyes fastened upon the emerald clock.

Twenty minutes of three! Twenty minutes, and then—! The little gnome fairly hugged himself with wicked anticipation. Ten minutes of three and now everything was in readiness. Dorothy and Betsy, giggling together, were putting the finishing touches to the table. The Scarecrow and Sir Hokus, between them, were composing a speech of welcome, for, of course, the Cowardly Lion had not been able to find the Patchwork Girl. Ranged about the walls in pleasant anticipation stood the courtiers and dear old celebrities of Oz. Nick Chopper, the Tin Woodman, summoned from his palace by the Wizard's magic, stood conversing in a low tone with Pastoria, Ozma's Royal Father, about his crop of tin cans, which were larger this year than ever before. The little Wizard of Oz, himself, was whispering to Tik Tok, the machine man, some of the tricks he was planning for the company's amusement and the metal man was chuckling with mechanical mirth. Hank, Betsy's mule, Toto, Dorothy's little dog, the Saw Horse, Ozma's Royal Steed, and all of the other palace pets were sitting expectantly at their own special table.

"Now then!" exclaimed the Scarecrow, having finished the speech of welcome to his own and the Knight's satisfaction, "as soon as I have finished this address, I shall extend a hand of

welcome to our little ruler, lead her triumphantly to the head of the table and—"

"Look!" rasped the Tin Woodman, who stood nearest the door. "Look! Look up! Look out!" Following the direction of Nick Chopper's tin finger everyone did look and, next minute, in fright and bewilderment, huddled together for protection, for over the heads flashed the hand of Kuma Party.

"The welcoming hand!" gasped the Scarecrow, clutching Sir Hokus. "But whose? Everybody count his hands," mumbled the Scarecrow, looking anxiously at his own.

"The hand that smote me," roared the Knight, making a lunge at the hand with his sword. Everyone else ducked, dodged and shuddered as the arm sailed hither and thither over their heads.

"It's a trick of the Wizard's," faltered Dorothy, looking hopefully at the little man. But the Wizard, peering palely from behind a huge green chair, shook his head positively.

"I had no hand in this," muttered the Wizard, mopping his bald head with his best hanky. Now, Kuma's hand could unfortunately carry out only the instructions given it by its owner. The note of warning for Ozma was tightly clasped in its fingers, but as Ozma was not present, it presumed she was to be found in another part of the palace and immediately flashed up the golden stairway in search of her and the invisible gnome. But Ruggedo was now more invisible than ever, having crawled under the table at the first sight of the flying arm. As the arm disappeared, everyone heaved a sigh of relief.

WIZ

"Come! Come!" wheezed the Wizard, stepping out nervously from behind the green chair, "we must not let a little thing like this spoil the party."

"Why, it's three o'clock now!"

"And here's Ozma!" cried Dorothy. And there, indeed, was Ozma, standing with a quiet smile in the doorway. At once the Scarecrow burst into his speech:

> "Welcome Ozma, beauteous Queen
> Sovereign of this City Green,
> Illustrious ruler—"

Thump! Ban—g! CRASH! With hand still upraised, the Scarecrow swung to the long French windows. So did everyone for that matter.

"A menagerie!" shrilled Nick Chopper, falling back against the wall.

"Why, it's Scraps!" burst out the Scarecrow, as the oztrich, with his three dusty riders, plunged giddily into the room.

"Beware!" roared the oztrich in a terrible voice, and when an oztrich roars it is four times louder than a lion. "Beware!"

Knocking over Tik Tok and three footmen, bearing trays of lemonade, the great green bird rushed impetuously toward the queen. "Beware!" it roared again so lustily that Ozma's curls blew straight out behind.

"Beware," coughed the Scarecrow irritably. "Well, I ought to be where you are. Out of my place, you rude monster."

"Beware the Gnome King!" finished the

oztrich, bowing his head so low and so suddenly that the Patchwork Girl fell off one side and Peter and Grumpy off the other.

CHAPTER 18

OZMA, surprised enough at the party, was so startled and dismayed by the oztrich's roars that she caught at a little gold stand to keep from falling. As she steadied herself, two arms clasped themselves round her waist.

"Oh! Oh! Someone is trying to steal my magic belt!" wailed the little fairy, swaying dizzily from side to side.

"Take this! Take this!" Bounding to his feet, Peter picked up the oztrich egg and fairly forced it into Ozma's arms. As he did so there came a blood-curdling screech, and then, perfect silence.

"It's Ruggedo!" puffed the Patchwork Girl, who had picked herself up by this time.

"Look for a blue patch! Look for a blue patch!" panted Grumpy, standing on his hind legs and sniffing the air anxiously. But there was no sign of a blue patch anywhere, for Ruggedo at the first glimpse of the egg had commanded the magic cloak to carry him to the royal stable. Here, trembling and shaken, he cowered in the Hungry Tiger's stall. Furious to have been frustrated by Peter at the very instant when success seemed sure, he raved and sputtered and tried to think up some way to get his belt in spite of the hateful egg.

Meanwhile, in the palace, the utmost confusion prevailed, and when the hand of Kuma again flashed into the banquet hall and flew like an arrow to Ozma and dropped the note of warning into her lap, the courtiers fled in every direction, while the celebrities crowded close about the little Queen to protect her from these confusing and invisible enemies.

"Stop! Stop!" panted Peter, as Sir Hokus, waving his sword, made determined swings at the flying arm. "It's a helping hand! It belongs to a friend of mine, Sir!" Tugging at the iron coat tails of the Knight, he sought to dissuade him from his grim purpose, but not until Ozma clapped sharply did the good Knight desist.

Leaning back wearily in the chair to which the Scarecrow had guided her, and still holding the great oztrich egg in her lap, Ozma turned to Scraps.

"What does this mean? Who are these strangers, and where is the Gnome King?" asked Ozma in a faint voice. As she spoke, Kuma's hand patted Peter approvingly on the head, and doubled into a fist under the Knight's nose and, sailing upward, settled quietly on the green chandelier.

> "I've been a Queen, I've riz and fell
> And have a thrilling tale to tell!"

puffed Scraps, tossing back her yarn dramatically.

"Never mind the thrills, come to the point! Come to the point!" growled the Cowardly Lion, looking uneasily at the oztrich, who was strutting pompously up and down the banquet hall, and at Grumpy, who was casting longing eyes at the banquet table.

Now the whole company turned expectantly to the Patchwork Girl and, enjoying the importance of her position and news to the very fullest extent, Scraps told her story and Peter's, while the little boy kept a sharp lookout for the invisible gnome. Scraps' own adventures were surprising enough, but when she came to Peter's experiences with the former Gnome King, the sea quakes, their escape in the pirate ship and the magic casket of Soob, the Sorcerer, the excitement of her hearers knew no bounds. Clapping on two pair of specs, the Wizard of Oz rushed from the room to fetch his encyclopedia of magic and his black bag, for he felt that his utmost skill would be needed to prevent the gnome from carrying out his wicked plans.

"It must have been Ruggedo who pinched you and pulled the Cowardly Lion's tail," whispered Dorothy, who was standing between Sir Hokus and the Scarecrow. When the good Knight heard how Kuma had dispatched his hand to aid Peter and Scraps in their escape from Patch, he waved apologetically at the arm resting on the chandelier. It at once descended and began shaking hands all around and Peter, staring at that gay and brilliant assemblage, thought he had never seen so interesting and strange a sight. The Hungry Tiger, now that the story was told, was all for going on with the party, but the Wizard, realizing the extreme danger they were in, said no.

"Put all the magic treasures together and place the oztrich egg on top of them," commanded the wizard, "for Ruggedo dare not touch them so long as the egg is near."

So Ozma unclasped her belt and, placing the oztrich egg in the center, put her magic box and wishing pills beside it.

"I cannot believe Ruggedo would be so wicked," sighed Ozma, turning sadly to the Scarecrow. "Now that he sees it is impossible to steal the belt perhaps he will go away."

"Not he!" answered the Scarecrow positively. "He's around here somewhere, depend on that, and until we find him, watch out!"

"Why not eat, while we watch?" purred the Hungry Tiger. "These travellers look tired and hungry and deserve refreshment after their long journey."

Grumpy rolled his eyes approvingly at the Hungry Tiger and Ozma, in spite of herself, had to smile. As she nodded her royal head, the Scarecrow burst into his speech of welcome all over again, the footmen began pulling out the chairs and everyone settled down as if nothing at all had happened. Grumpy had a place between the Hungry Tiger and Cowardly Lion, and they, well pleased with the behavior of the little bear, did their best to make him feel at home. The oztrich stood up behind

Grumpy, swallowing rapidly everything that came within reach. Scraps had the seat of honor beside Ozma, and Peter, between Dorothy and Sir Hokus, was plied with every delicacy. The hand of Kuma, trained to serve, flew backward and forward, filling tumblers, carrying trays and generally making itself useful.

"Dost like our Emerald City, lad?" queried Sir Hokus, bending kindly toward the little boy.

"Well," acknowledged Peter quite truthfully, "I haven't seen much of it, the oztrich ran so fast, you know."

"A rare and exceptional bird!" murmured Sir Hokus mildly, "but not my idea of a giddy steed."

"Nor mine!" whispered Peter, winking sociably at the Knight. "He goes twenty feet at one jump and travels like a hurricane." Between bites, Peter told the Knight how they had run over the bookman and a little more about the pirate ship and the Sultan of Suds, while Scraps, at the head of the table, gave a spirited account of her experiences as Queen of the Quilties.

So light hearted and gay are these dear people of Oz that soon they were laughing and chatting as merrily as if no danger threatened their little ruler or themselves. Only the Wizard seemed to be bothering about the Gnome King. He had

placed his encyclopedia beside him on the table and, nibbling absently at a chicken leg, continued to pore over its finely printed pages in an effort to trace the magic articles Peter had found in the sorcerer's chest. It must be confessed that Peter glanced from time to time at the chair where the magic belt lay, marveling at its wonderful powers and hoping that when everything was over it would safely transport him back to Philadelphia.

"After the party we'll have the Cowardly Lion take us all over the Emerald City," promised Dorothy, as Peter dipped his spoon into a heaping saucer of Ozcream. Blissfully, Peter nodded, then glanced again at the magic belt, dropped his spoon with a crash and pushed back his chair.

"The egg!" gasped Peter wildly. "It's hatched!" And it most certainly had! As the startled company sprang to their feet, the baby oztrich stepped awkwardly out of its shell, wobbled to the edge of the chair and fell off. And that was not all! For as the oztrich, with great strides, rushed to the side of its child, the magic belt, the box of wishing pills and the magic box disappeared and a blue patch began to flutter and dance before the horrified eyes of the now thoroughly alarmed guests of Ozma.

"The Gnome King!" groaned the Wizard, slamming his book with a bang.

"The belt!" screamed Peter, dashing toward the blue patch. Feeling that something might happen that would enable him to carry out his plans, Ruggedo had returned to the banquet hall and, watching from a safe distance, saw to his utter relief and astonishment that the egg had hatched. Instantly its power over him ceased and, dashing forward, he had pounced upon the belt and clasped it about his waist.

"Revenge!" roared the voice of the invisible gnome. "Revenge! Next moment I shall send you all to the bottom of the Nonestic Ocean!"

"Not that! Not that!" faltered the Patchwork Girl, clutching Ozma in a panic. "I never could stand water!"

The Wizard Makes the Gnome King Visible

CHAPTER 19

AT Ruggedo's words, the celebrities and courtiers clung shuddering together. Knowing the awful power of the belt and feeling that they were indeed lost, they waited for the Gnome King to speak. But Peter, seizing first a tumbler, then a plate, sent them flying at the blue patch. Ruggedo might be invisible, but he was still there. Shaking his head angrily as the tumbler broke over his crown he cried in a loud voice, "I command you to transport—"

The plate, crashing against his nose, made him pause, and Peter followed this with a vase and water pitcher. But gnomes have hard heads and, with an angry roar, Ruggedo began again, "I command you to transport these people—"

By this time Peter had thrown everything in reach. Feeling desperately in his pocket he sent a top, a baseball and a box of fish hooks whizzing through the air. Then, as his fingers closed on the sorcerer's stone, he flung that, too, at the invisible gnome. Instantly there was a complete and utter silence. The patch still fluttered wildly before their eyes and, as the stunned company eyed it in horrified suspense, the hand of Kuma descended and closed roughly on the invisible shoulder of Ruggedo.

"Hold him! Hold him!" panted the Wizard, rushing forward with his black bag. "I remember now the magic to make him visible." The little Wizard of Oz seldom uses chants and, instead of the verse Wumbo had employed, sprinkled a black and white powder over the Gnome King. Even years afterward Peter could remember the distorted and furious face of Ruggedo, as the spell of the magic cloak was broken and he stood revealed to his enemies. Struggling to shake off the clutch of Kuma's hand, he was desperately trying to speak to the magic belt. But, though his mouth moved, not a sound issued from his lips.

"Struck dumb!" cried the Scarecrow, unclasping his arms from the Knight's neck, where he had flung them in his extreme agitation. "But how! And why?"

"I have it! I have it!" exclaimed the Wizard, pouncing upon the emerald that Peter, as a last resort, had hurled at the Gnome King. "This is the famous Silence Stone, used by the ancient Emperors of Oz to keep their wives quiet in times of war. How it came into the possession of Soob I cannot imagine, but see, here written in magic on the emerald itself is the whole story: 'Whom this stone touches on the head shall remain silent for seven years'."

"Yon honest lad hath saved the realm!" boomed Sir Hokus, slapping Peter on the back and beaming joyfully upon the still trembling company.

"I wish I could have read that before," puffed Peter.

"Well, it's lucky you threw it when you did," answered the Wizard. "One more word and we'd have been at the bottom of the sea. As it is—" Calmly the wizard unclasped the belt from the scowling Gnome King and, snatching the box of mixed magic and the wishing pills, handed them back to Ozma—"As it is, Ruggedo is perfectly harmless."

"Three cheers for Peter!" cried the Scarecrow, waving his hat over his head. "His aim and arm have saved the day."

"That's because he's such a good pitcher," mumbled the little bear, and the cheers were given with such a will all the dishes on the table skipped. Ozwold, who had buried his head in a flower pot at the first of the Gnome King's threats, now reared it cautiously and, with mud still sticking to his bill, approached the Queen.

"If Your Highness will excuse me," quavered the oztrich hoarsely, "I must be going. This excitement is very bad for my child."

Plucking a plume from his tail, Ozwold extended it politely. Smiling kindly, Ozma took the plume and sent Jellia, her little maid, to fetch an emerald necklace, for Scraps had, just in time, reminded her of the hatchday present for the baby oztrich.

"This is simply magnif—!" murmured Ozwold and, as Ozma fastened the necklace round his long neck, the company cheered and cheered again, for they felt that the great green bird was in a large measure responsible for their safety. Ozwold, himself, was anxious to turn his child over to his wife and tell her the story of his amazing adventures, so Dorothy and Peter placed the baby oztrich on his back, fastening it securely with a hair ribbon. Nodding stiffly to the right and left, Ozwold strutted proudly from the banquet hall, and immediately the Ozites surrounded Peter, congratulating and praising him, till the little boy grew quite red with embarrassment and pleasure.

At Ozma's command, Ruggedo was led away to the cellar and, with nothing more to worry them or mar the festivities, the party began again and lasted far into the night. The Emerald Palace is so large and so roomy that none of the guests thought of going home and, after the Wizard had performed the last of his tricks and Scraps had recited the funniest of her verses, they all trooped off to bed, calling cheerily to each other as they mounted the golden stairs. Peter had a royal suite to himself and, curling down luxuriously in the grand gold bed, wondered if he were not already asleep and dreaming of all this magnificence. A bare little room had been found for Grumpy, and the little bear, well pleased with his new quarters and comrades, was soon asleep and snoring tremendously.

Peter Is Made a Prince of Oz

CHAPTER 20

WITH Scraps and Dorothy for guides and the Cowardly Lion and Hungry Tiger for steeds, Peter and Grumpy rode over the whole Emerald City next morning, receiving everywhere the cheers and acclaim of the inhabitants. The story of Peter's prowess had gone abroad and he was everywhere hailed as the hero of the hour. Right after breakfast, he had written a long note to Kuma, telling him the whole story of Ruggedo's treachery and thanking him for his great generosity. Kuma's arm, which had needed for the night only a little elbow room, immediately flew back to its master, with the note and a great bag of emeralds sent by Ozma to express her thanks and appreciation.

Luncheon was another party, but, as Dorothy and Betsy explained to the little boy, every day in the Emerald City is just like one big party.

"Do stay here!" urged Dorothy and, Ozma herself, coming to Peter's chair, begged him to make his home in the marvelous land of Oz.

"You shall be a Prince!" promised Ozma graciously, "and rule over one of our smaller Kingdoms. Prince Peter the First, how is that?" The celebrities waved and cheered at Ozma's words, and Peter, seeing that everyone expected it, rose to make the most important speech of his life.

"I'd like to stay and be a Prince," said Peter slowly, "but you see, folks, I'm a pitcher and I couldn't go back on the fellows and on my grandfather, so if your Majesty will just transport me to Philadelphia, why that will be reward enough."

"Spoken like a true and loyal Knight!" cried Sir Hokus, thumping on the table.

"Good-night!" sighed Scraps, for she had taken a great fancy to Peter, and had rather hoped he would stay in Oz.

"Would you like to go now?" asked Ozma, with a merry smile, for Ozma had a little plan of her own. Peter nodded a little bashfully, for it did seem a bit rude to want to leave so delightful a place and company, but he felt that he ought to get in a little practice for the game. So Ozma immediately put on her magic belt and, extending her right hand, said, imperiously:

"I command you to transport this boy and the pirate's gold to Philadelphia!" Instantly

Peter vanished and the Ozites, running up the stairs two at a time, crowded round the magic picture in Ozma's sitting room.

"Show us Peter," panted Ozma, for she was a little out of breath from her run. At her words the country scene in the picture faded and there *was* Peter, sitting in the middle of a dusty ball field, with a bag of gold on each side, and a crowd of cheering boys around him.

"I thought some of that gold might be real!" exclaimed Ozma, turning triumphantly to the Wizard. "Polacky must have been a real pirate before he sailed into the Nonestic Ocean and while I could not transport any of our gold or jewels to Philadelphia, two bags of the pirate's gold were real."

"Oh! Won't he have fun!" squealed Dorothy, giving Scraps a hug.

That night Peter, sitting on the arm of his grandfather's chair, had the pleasure of seeing in the evening paper the heading he had thought up himself:

"Philadelphia Boy Finds Treasure and Saves the Emerald City of Oz."

Back in the capital there were only a few things to settle now. The Silence Stone and Magic Cloak were carefully stored away in the emerald safe in the Wizard's laboratory to be used in case of extreme danger or war.

Kaliko was at once notified of Ruggedo's capture and permitted to resume his place as King of the Gnomes.

Walking in the garden, the same afternoon that Peter had been sent back to Philadelphia, the Wizard of Oz had noticed a gold thread running under one of the benches. Following it curiously he found that it led into the palace, up the stairs to the very top sunny chamber where an old Winkie Woman named Susan Smiggs did all the palace mending. Susan, then, was the proper ruler of Patch, and Scraps, shaking her head dubiously, watched the fat little seamstress drive away in the Red Wagon, to take up her duties as Queen of the Quilties. But as Ozma had promised to revise the laws of Patch, perhaps Susan will have a better time than the Patchwork Girl did.

As for Ruggedo, deciding that the loss of speech for seven years was punishment enough, Ozma kindly granted the gnome his freedom, first taking the precaution to have him dipped into the fountain of Oblivion. As anyone touched by these waters forgets all his past wickedness, let us hope that from now on Ruggedo will lead a better life and cause no more trouble in Oz.

THE INTERNATIONAL WIZARD OF OZ CLUB

The International Wizard of Oz Club was founded in 1957 to bring together all those interested in Oz, its authors and illustrators, film and stage adaptations, toys and games, and associated memorabilia. From a charter group of 16, the club has grown until today it has over 1800 members of all ages throughout the world. Its magazine, *The Baum Bugle*, first appeared in June 1957 and has been published continuously ever since. The *Bugle* appears three times a year and specializes in popular and scholarly articles about Oz and its creators, biographical and critical studies, first edition checklists, research into the people and places within the Oz books, etc. The magazine is illustrated with rare photographs and drawings, and the covers are in full color. The Oz Club also publishes a number of other Oz-associated items, including full-color maps; an annual collection of original Oz stories; books; and essays.

Each year, the Oz Club sponsors conventions in different areas of the United States. These gatherings feature displays of rare Oz and Baum material, an Oz quiz, showings of Oz films, an auction of hard-to-find Baum and Oz items, much conversation about Oz in all its aspects, and many other activities.

The International Wizard of Oz Club appeals to the serious student and collector of Oz as well as to any reader interested in America's own fairyland. For further information, please send a *long* self-addressed stamped envelope to:

Fred M. Meyer, Executive Secretary
THE INTERNATIONAL WIZARD
OF OZ CLUB
Box 95
Kinderhook, IL 62345